Praise for Samar Yazbek

"One of Syria's most gifted

CNN

"Yazbek's is the urgent task of showing the world what is happening. Thanks to her, we can read about the appalling things that go on in secret, underground places."

The Guardian

•

Praise for Where the Wind Calls Home

"From the simple story of a soldier who is subjected to friendly fire and relives moments from the span of his life as he hovers between life and death, Yazbek conveys to her reader the true story that constitutes the novel within her novel: the story of nature merging with a person more like a son to her, at the fateful moment when his feelings open up to their full truth. This story is represented in a unique manner through the condensing and stretching of time; written in language filled with eloquent poetry and vernacular vitality that moves with the pulse of the people; varying the narrative time between past, present and future; creating a structure that accommodates the two overlapping narratives; and choosing unique, captivating characters through which events and history are set in motion, references and traits are created, and selves are made both simpler and more complex."

Al-Quds Al-Arabi

“*A* story about the relationship between humanity and violence, and the imagination’s ability to save us from the hell of the present.”
Iraqpalm

“Yazbek’s language is distinguished by the power of her phrasing, the eloquence of her vocabulary, drawing on an abundant linguistic store, encyclopedic knowledge, and culture, and the accumulation of personal experience.”
EREM News

“Samar Yazbek has written a powerful, symphonic novel, in language that is flowing, sharp, and precise. It has a leisurely rhythm and a transparent beauty. A novel that, one wishes, one was not reading through the lens of scrutiny, but with the anesthetic of hope and the purity of wishful thinking.”
Independent Arabia

•

Praise for Planet of Clay

“The young, mute narrator of this compassionate novel becomes a poignant emblem of the Syrian women confined by war … A bold portrayal of besieged people.”
The Observer

“*Planet of Clay* is a devastating novel about human resilience and fragility in a time of war.”
Foreword Reviews, starred review

"Rima is a fantastic character."
Kirkus Reviews

"*Planet of Clay* gives a haunting and unflinching look at the horrors of war—the bombing, the starvation, the fear—all seen through the eyes of Rima, a young girl with a vibrant imagination."
NPR

"Wrenching ... offers a remarkable account of wartime despair."
Publishers Weekly

"Samar Yazbek has written a novel that manages to speak to the urgency of telling and listening to the most vulnerable of stories—stories by people who in other circumstances might have had more than one story to tell."
Words Without Borders

"Dealing with themes that are close to the author's heart, Yazbek brilliantly weaves a story about freedom and of heartbreak during wartime."
Arab News

"The Syrian writer Samar Yazbek evokes the horror of civil war with gripping lucidity in her novel *Planet of Clay.*"
Le Monde

"With the brazenness typical of her recent work, Samar Yazbek immerses us in the horror of the Syrian conflict,

and the way it resonates in the flesh and minds of those who are living it. It is through the women the author has met on the ground throughout this war that she describes the capacity for resistance in the face of atrocity."
Libération

"An ingenious character and a literary approach on the verge of the unimaginable. Samar Yazbek's novel is brave on many levels."
Göteborgs-Posten

"*Planet of Clay* is a deeply original, almost surreal fantasia, written in a simple, clear style. But the evil and the suffering surrounding Rima are so very real. A novel like *Planet of Clay* filters through all our conscious and unconscious blinkers."
Arbetarbladet

"The rest of us can only read—and cry."
Kristeligt Dagblad

"The book left this reader very touched, beyond the cruel reality it describes, thanks to Yazbek's sensitivity towards detail."
Weekendavisen

"An invaluable voice from Syria."
Dagens Nyheter

"The text is true—literally true, that is. How can you truly describe rational chemical warfare? By letting the

process supporting the meaning of the text break down. A radical and visionary move made by Samar Yazbek."
Sveriges Radio

•

Praise for A Woman in the Crossfire: Diaries of the Syrian Revolution

"Amid the horrific news about Syrian dissidents, mass killings, and government claims of terrorists, this unique document, written in the first months of the uprising, is a chronicle both of objective events and the visceral and psychic responses of an impassioned activist and artist. The book weaves journalistic reporting into intimate, poetic musings on an appalling reality."
Publishers Weekly

"An essential eyewitness account, and with luck an inaugural document in a Syrian literature that is uncensored and unchained."
Kirkus Reviews

"A feverish, nightmarish, immediate account."
The Guardian

"An impassioned and harrowing memoir of the early revolt."
New York Review of Books

"In her book, *Woman in the Crossfire: Diaries of the Syrian Revolution*, Yazbek shows the reality of what's happening there and brings us stories of the many people who risk their lives in the struggle for freedom. The insight that she offers into the complex and bloody conflict is both incredibly valuable and inspiring."
PEN Transmissions

"The best account of the revolution's early months."
The National

"Arresting, novelistic prose. Uncompromising reportage from a doomed capital."
The Spectator

"The heartbreaking diary of a woman who risked her life to document the regime's brutal attacks on peaceful demonstrators."
The Inquirer

"A remarkable, devastating account of the three increasingly dangerous trips that Yazbek made to northern Syria in 2012 and 2013, sneaking over the Turkish border each time."
The Nation

"Poetic prose and gritty reportage successfully combine to create a terrifying picture of a woman whose body and soul are tortured by her experience of the uprising."
Syrian Observer

•

Praise for The Crossing: My Journey to the Shattered Heart of Syria

"A powerful and moving account of her devastated homeland. It bears comparison with George Orwell's *Homage to Catalonia* as a work of literature. Yazbek is a superb narrator. One of the first political classics of the twenty-first century."
The Guardian

"Extraordinarily powerful, poignant and affecting. I was greatly moved."
MICHAEL PALIN

"Brave, rebellious and passionate. Yazbek is no ordinary Syrian dissident."
Financial Times

"An eloquent, gripping and harrowing account of the country's decline into barbarism by an incredibly brave Syrian."
Irish Times

"Gripping. Does the important job of putting faces to the numbing numbers of Syria's crisis."
The Economist

"Samar Yazbek's searing new book about her Syrian homeland is a testament to the indomitable spirit of her countrymen in their struggle against the Assad regime. Shocking, searing, and beautiful."
Daily Beast

Where the Wind Calls Home

Samar Yazbek

Where the Wind Calls Home

Translated from the Arabic by Leri Price

WORLD EDITIONS
New York

Published in the USA in 2023 by World Editions NY LLC

World Editions
New York

Printed by Lightning Source, USA

Library of Congress Cataloging in Publication Data is available

ISBN 978-1-64286-135-8

First published as *Maqam al Rih* in Arabic in 2021 by Manshourat al mutawassit, Milano

Company: worldeditions.org
Facebook: @WorldEditionsInternationalPublishing
Instagram: @WorldEdBooks
TikTok: @worldeditions_tok
Twitter: @WorldEdBooks
YouTube: World Editions

Chapter 1

Just a small leaf. He couldn't see it through his tangled lashes, beneath the midday sun.

A leaf, nothing more. Lobed and green, it appeared in front of his eyes like a curtain each time he slowly and laboriously moved his eyelids. A leaf brushing his long, mud-spattered lashes. A leaf only vaguely visible through the soft grains of soil swimming in the water of his eyes, chafing and burning. If he opened his eyelids again, the leaf would fall into his left eye. That leaf was the entire world. No sound, no smell. He couldn't feel his other eye. Was he still alive? Did he have a body? If so, where was it? His sense of existence extended no further than the narrow strip of faint light hidden behind these black lines—he didn't care whether they were his eyelashes or his nightmares, in any case the darkness would soon settle within once more. He was slowly falling into some deep and unknown place. His gravity was negated and he could feel his head swinging—perhaps he was falling into a grave. Was this his funeral? Was this his head?

The leaf fell and he could see an eye—his eye, wandering in the air, watching a body plunge into a hole. He couldn't see his body inside the coffin (though he knew it was his body), and the hole wasn't deep enough for him to be afraid, but it was deep enough for the disintegration and eventual disappearance that would take place after the soil was piled upon it. Thus, a single eye.

He envied the silhouettes of the people hovering around the hole. He found the sensation of swinging in a chasm very pleasant. He glimpsed the delicate roots of the grass branching out through the layers of soil, their roots, white, fine, and dense, destroyed by shovels. And he smelled dawn coming off the root tips, and he saw some pink worms tumbling over the edges of the coffin, and he recalled how yielding they were when he used to toy with them between his fingers. Where did that happen? When was it he collected some worms, lined them up on a large rock, and set them off on a race? He couldn't remember. But seeing the dancing worms accompany him as he fell, he was comforted—and then the vision dissolved. This was the burial ground next to the maqam and its giant tree. Was he still here? Where? What was "here"? It was him and no one else, unseparate from his existence. He saw himself as an observing eye. He could see the women gathering behind the men in the graveyard, their heads covered with white veils. He spotted one woman snatching her white scarf off her head, pushing forward between the men and shouting. It was his mother. How did he know? He couldn't see her clearly. So, he had a family. But he didn't feel anything. He was like a bird soaring, yet when he saw his family below, he knew he was not a bird. He was nothing more than a single eye (not even a pair of eyes) and he could see forms in all of their three dimensions. He was an eye hovering over the burial ground of the village (it was his village), and he saw himself going down into the hole, and he heard the sound of wailing and saw the silhouette of a woman; he believed it was his mother from her familiar acrobatic movements, the leaps that looked like indignation. The sound of ululation and howling, the firing of bullets, murmurings: these were familiar sounds at funerals. He couldn't hear the customary weeping and lamentations, and he couldn't see any women tearing at their clothes. He believed this scene wasn't unfamiliar to him—he had heard it and seen it at some earlier point in time—but the sound of commotion that followed afterwards seemed of a different kind. The man over there was his father, and there was his widowed sister with her swollen belly, but his vision was hazy because he was hovering above them and couldn't come down to earth. He was an eye flying in the air, descending to see if this funeral was for him or his brother.

He failed to move and establish who the grave belonged to, as he was braced in the sky by unseen ropes. Below him, the assembled crowd paused, then drifted off in various directions; they were moving their lips, although he couldn't hear what they were saying. He wanted to scream, to say that he was still here, he hadn't died, he didn't want to die—he would have liked to tell them that it was some monster going down into that hole, or perhaps a stranger, *not him*, but no one was listening. He recognised this funeral but, as he repeated crossly to himself, he couldn't work out whether it was his brother's funeral or his own. He looked around and saw other human body parts also bound by invisible ropes in the sky. These body parts were staring at the many holes that filled up the mountaintops overlooking the sea. He choked briefly and his head cleared a little: how could an eye choke?

He was just a single eye looking at a hole. Finally he could hear his mother sing. That was her voice! At times his mother sang, and at other times she let out piercing groans. He saw her shout and knew she was screaming his name, but he couldn't hear her. The sound disappeared when she called him. She was looking at the sky; she knew that he was looking at her. His mother's voice was calling him—this meant that he was dead and observing his own soul swinging in the sky. He wanted to whistle so his mother would recognise him, but he was just an eye, and in no position to imitate a blackbird as he used to do. And he saw the flag very clearly: red white black, with two stars in the middle. What colour were the stars? He didn't know. Then he saw his mother's hands grab the coffin and pull off the flag. Her chapped fingers had transformed into a giant screen implanted into the wood, as inextricably part of the coffin as its nails. Then sound and colour disappeared while his mother's body remained attached to the coffin. He realised he wasn't dead, because he remembered at a certain point—at the point he moved his eyelids and saw the leaf—that this funeral was for his brother, and the person he could see going down into the hole was not him. Then he opened his other eye and saw again. The leaf had lurched and fallen off his face, and vision unfurled before him. He discovered that his head was still securely on top of his body, and that the leaf (along with other leaves) covered as much of his body as he could feel. He was able to move his head again and see the tree. A huge tree, that seemed far away, yet not far away enough to be a figment of his imagination, that was neither a dream nor a nightmare. His squinting eyes widened and all of a sudden brightness flooded him. He was alive, and had been here recently. He wasn't sure exactly when, but it was certainly here. He was flooded by the sky overhead and the leaves ... yellow and grey and crumbling. There was a single green leaf in front of his left eye. There was no sound. Absolute silence. It was at that moment he realised he couldn't move, that he could smell a familiar, burning odour, and that he had two hands, because he could feel them. Then he heard the rustling of the leaves as they disintegrated, and he shook his body in a feeble movement, which only resulted in the discovery that his other eye could also see. From the viewpoint of someone looking down from the sky, his body must look like a heap of leaves and branches, a mask of mud and blood with two eyeholes obtruding on top. Only the whites of his eyes would betray that there was a human body on this desolate void of a mountaintop, towered over by a huge tree.

He hadn't known it until that moment. Hadn't realised he was buried beneath leaves and soil and branches. He was aware only that he was breathing and that he had two eyes and two hands. Then he heard his heartbeat, and he let out a deep sigh that stirred the bones in his chest, and he heard the rustling sound again. He was still here, above the earth, but he couldn't feel his feet and a skewer of fire was crippling his back. Or perhaps it was a skewer of ice—but it burned. He didn't know what it was; it felt sticky, as if he was buried up to his chest in cement. He couldn't get up to inspect his body, but he still believed he was alive.

He was confused by the presence of the tree. Perhaps it was the tree by the village maqam, or the tree by their house. And perhaps he was whoever was being lowered into the hole; he wasn't certain of his imaginings, despite recalling that it was his brother's funeral. It was the same tree he had known from childhood. He remembered, after an hour of sweating and staring into the sun, which was climbing higher in the sky, that the tree was here, on the frontline, and that he had been here, looking at it, entranced as usual, holding his rifle, and the other soldiers in his unit had been standing next to him.

He decided to move, despite being briefly tempted to fall into the lethargy of the abyss. So he shook his body again, only to realise that he couldn't move. The surrounding silence frightened him—he could hear only his own heartbeats, which almost burst his eardrums. Where was this silence coming from? Where were the sounds of the birds and the trees? *Every tree must have its own voice, and the voices of its companions, the birds.* Who had said that to him? To the right of the tree he noticed thick smoke rising, and when he directed his gaze to the left, he saw fire. Something was burning, and he could smell barbecued meat. He closed his eyes. It was a scorching noon, its intensity broken only by the mountain air. Drops of sweat gushed over his forehead; they soaked his eyelashes, burned his eyes, then stopped him seeing anything at all for a few minutes. He decided to try breathing deeply in order to feel his stomach muscles and force himself to move. His chest rose and fell as he breathed in and out, and the pile of leaves rose with it. He was able to shift slightly and turn over part of himself, and, with excruciating slowness, was able to move his torso at last. When he forced himself in the other direction, he reflected that maybe the abyss lay there and the edge not far away, but he ignored it. He was propelled by a prodigious force from his very guts, but afterwards all he had to show for it was that he had turned onto his side and was now face-to-face with the tree. The leaves and branches slid off his chest and he instantly felt a searing pain which struck him with the sudden hope that he was whole. The pain circulated from his head to his toes and he felt it through his whole body: an excellent sign, in his view. He turned his head, keeping his eyes fixed on the tree, and heard rustling and the snapping of dry twigs. Then silence fell again and he saw an image of himself and the other soldiers flying through the air as the bomb exploded. Before unconsciousness returned he heard his mother's hoarse voice calling him: *Ali!* Then he knew, was certain, that this small green leaf came from an oak tree.

Chapter 2

No sooner had he been pulled in by sluggishness, drowning in misery and lethargy, than the voice shouted his name and plucked him out of his surrender. The voice lifted him, and he lifted his head as he heard a fierce whisper in his ear. The sky was blue and it mingled with occasional and distant clouds that journeyed one by one directly above his eyes. A few days ago he had spotted the clouds that sped between him and the other soldiers. There had been five of them in total, and he was the only one who knew the states and transformations of the clouds: how they deceived and twisted, how they could dampen his breath. The clouds had been his playthings from the rooftop of his house, his companions along the rugged mountain paths. Today, the clouds seemed different, both near and far at the same time. They used to cover him like a blanket for days at a time, or they would moisten his eyelids, as if he could reach out and touch them. He imagined how his fingers would lengthen and grow alongside them like buds breaking into leaf, unfolding and transforming into branches that covered the mountaintop. He liked to reach his head among the clouds and twist and turn in their whiteness like he was taking a bath. He would rub his face in them as he used to do in the snow. He would grab hold of them and his fingers would merge with the blankness. And then he would smile inwardly and see the whiteness of his smile inside him—he would leave himself. He would make himself dizzy with clouds despite the warnings from the other soldiers, whom he secretly scorned. He was an expert in the states of the clouds, and according to his reckoning they would never betray him. He stood in front of the other soldiers as the dense white flocks covered them all, chewing on a void in his mouth, trusting that their soft succulence would enter his throat and bring him quietly to sleep, as it always used to do on the cold nights in his arzal and on the rooftop. But now he wasn't on the rooftop, or in his arzal—he was on an unfamiliar mountain peak which seemed to him like a bald, scabby head. It was utterly desolate on this summit, apart from that giant tree and the ramparts made of sandbags.

The clouds here were not like the clouds in his village, the clouds he had lived among and knew so well. The clouds he knew floated upwards from the bottom of the valley, and he saw them as a thick white river that covered all the world around him until they enveloped him completely and stopped up his vision. The villagers had always lived alongside mist and clouds and were accustomed to disappearing within them, while Ali had made them into his own cloud river. That cloud river, alone, would turn into a long tail, shaking and twitching as he watched, like the tail of a mountain fox. He'd stand in his arzal, gazing until it disappeared, and he would see how the valley and neighbouring mountain peaks appeared sparkling clean as soon as that foxtail of white had dissolved, and he would leap for joy knowing that the tail would wind back around all the way up to his own mountain peak, where it would be waiting for him as he wrapped himself up in his mother's quilt. There were worlds like these that were all his own, ones it was impossible for anyone to discover inside him, his alone that no one else could reach—such as when he would stay on a tree branch for hours, folding his legs like a heron, looking out over all that majesty, straining his eyes and repeating in wonder, "*Ya waily, ya waila* ..." Whenever the sky was murky grey, illuminated columns suddenly appeared amid the darkness, connecting the earth to the sky like huge ropes of light. He would bend his head to see the grey clouds that kept moving along, and he would sail alongside them and those shining columns, and meanwhile the grey clouds scattered and made space for the released light. He would see a carnival of interwoven colours—grey, blue, black, yellow—colours undulating and entwining, creating shapes through perpetual motion, and he thought this must be paradise. Colours overwhelmed him. Then there came those shapes created by the clouds in the guise of strange, living creatures: he seemed to glimpse the face of a woman with the body of a tree whose branches ended in small feet; or a tree with cow legs and a pair of hands formed from hundreds of butterflies; or a bird crowned by goat horns, with wings made of branches and a pair of human feet. Those cloud formations in all their magnificence would disperse before his eyes and transform into soft, small fragments of flock, while he remained standing there, watching till they disappeared, feeling a bottomless pit inside him. He didn't know if it was a pit of joy, or fear, or wonder ... or what? So he would climb down from the tree and stagger away, filled with light. He seemed to be one with those clouds, and something in his head would disperse, just like the clouds themselves. He wouldn't even realise that dark had fallen. From those moments, he had learned that everything around him would disappear, just like those giant clouds—even Ali himself would disappear, he could feel it happening sometimes. Inwardly, he thought of it as the clouds' work, making him like them.

On this day the clouds were far away and wouldn't rescue him; they continued on their way and disappeared, leaving him alone. He wished one of them would roll over him, but that seemed like an impossible dream.

The disc of the sun prevented him from opening his eyelids much, but when with some effort he was able to open his eyes, the light ambushed him and the silence took on a whispering tone. Then he raised his head and turned his gaze away from the sky and towards the tree; he heard his name being repeated and the whispering was broken. He raised his upper half and craned his head upwards, shaking off the leaves and dust and soil, and then the voice came back, hoarse, as it was earlier—his mother's voice! He realised he had forgotten her name, although he remembered that he used to know it. Sluggish and weary, he turned his head to find her. He bit his tongue to achieve sensation of any kind until the pain overcame him suddenly, and there was a salty taste in his mouth.

Ali!

The voice sounded clear this time, and he remembered seeing her walking with a few other women behind the crowd of men. Eyes glued to her, he saw her trip and fall and he watched as her neighbours, black-wrapped and still wailing, rose to help her. The whole crowd formed a long line as they walked slowly and surely along the village paths, the men at the front carrying the bier. He could see it all clearly. He was pulling his mother's skinny, broken-down body away from the men's procession as it carried on without them. This was their second funeral. A month had passed since they buried his sister's husband, although that funeral he couldn't quite remember. The day in his mind now, which he saw and remembered clearly, wasn't a dream. It had been his brother's funeral. Yes, it was his brother's funeral, and he himself was still alive, and the light that collided with him when he opened his eyes was nothing other than reality. He was still on earth, and he wasn't yet dead—he was still living, still seeing these images. The villagers had gathered in front of the new burial ground. At that time, the country was inventing strange new kinds of burial grounds, some open and visible, and others more covert; small ones where dismembered body parts were buried, and giant ones with room for hundreds of people in a single grave. In their villages they used to stumble upon stone burial grounds that went back thousands of years. Decades earlier the villagers used to bury their dead by their houses, and every house had its graves. They used to live alongside their dead in the small spaces afforded by the mountain slope. On that fearsome mountain slope, it was said, were the graves of three revolutionaries who had fought against the French. And facing their house, where thirty years ago a huge, high-walled palace had appeared, was a burial ground that was different again. The man who owned the palace had fashioned a mausoleum and buried his father there, then his men had announced that this tomb was now a new maqam for the village. The villagers secretly whispered among themselves, wondering how the owner of the palace, a high-ranking army officer called Abu Zayn, could have created a new maqam! In any case, it wasn't important because the villages rarely sought blessings there, and the story had no interest for Ali now as he became aware of his name and saw an image of his mother and the funeral. He didn't know anything about the owner of the palace apart from the fact that he had wanted to make his father into a saint; some of the villagers used to snigger in mockery of this narrative, and others would dutifully repeat tales of the father's virtuous deeds and how he had entered the ranks of God's saints. What Ali did know was that his brother had gone to see Abu Zayn in Damascus and the officer had helped him enlist in the army, and that this same high-ranking officer hadn't a square foot of land in the village when he was young, and now owned most of it. This meant little to Ali – and to the owner of the palace. This man wasn't particularly attached to the stony ground, having left his village some half-century earlier and settled in Damascus, only to return to his birthplace a few years ago bearing the moniker of the "old guard," a club whose services had been dismissed upon the death of the previous President and the arrival of the new guard. Most of the villagers knew that the "old guard" belonged to the late President, and certainly *not* to his son, the current President. The owner of the palace, Abu Zayn, who (it was said) resented the manner in which he had been expelled from the intelligence services, was not at the funeral with the villagers but sent his son Zayn in his stead. When Ali saw Zayn for the first time he was terrified; at the funeral Ali remembered him and saw that his father was also looking at Al-Zayn with recognition. "Al-Zayn"—this was what others had to call him, with the definite article. Ali stole a glance at his mother, in the back with the other women. He walked and walked; the road to the Graveyard of Martyrs seemed never-ending. This was the new graveyard created especially for the soldiers killed in the war, because the village's original burial ground had been filled with the bodies of its youth and children and there wasn't an inch of space left. In this, it was no different from the other villages in the mountains and on the plains by the sea. The same scene was repeated there too. Graveyards started to appear and they were all given the same name: the Graveyard of Martyrs. On that rainy winter's day they were heading to the Graveyard of Martyrs, climbing the northern road all the way to the end where a small dusty plot of land faced the village on the opposite mountain slope. This plot was owned by a farmer, whose son—and his sons after him—had become high-up bureaucrats and only ever appeared in public in luxury cars with tinted windows. The villagers called this functionary "the security official." He had fled the village then returned as an old man during the war. He donated some land to establish the Graveyard of the Martyrs, and then he and his sons joined the militias that were proliferating in the mountains and on the plains at an incomprehensible rate. None of the farmers were at the funeral with the villagers. Instead, they were busy putting up checkpoints between villages, and stopping cars and arresting people ... and God only knew what else, according to the neighbours.

The entire village had turned out behind the bier, moving along in a wedding procession, and the zagharit of the women alternated with the shots fired by the men. The commanding officer had come to say a few words about the "Nation's Martyr," as he called Ali's brother. No one was allowed to see the body. They said this usually happened when the bodies were mutilated or in pieces; they put whatever bits they could find inside a wooden coffin and topped it up with sand, and the families were forbidden from opening it as they carried it from the hospital to the martyr's house, and from there to the maqam. The villagers believed that the souls of their dead had a duty to visit the house and stay there until their new member arrived, and the souls would then accompany the body on its burial journey. But that day, they took his brother's coffin directly to the graveyard and the villagers whispered to each other that his brother's body only consisted of a few tattered shreds, and so the commanding officer had given the order to proceed straight to the burial.

His mother collapsed, then stood up again, gazing all the while at the coffin being carried on the shoulders of the village's youth. She pleaded desperately for a final look at her son to bid him goodbye but the men, aghast, merely uttered, "*Astaghfirullah,*" shook their heads, and ignored her. As for the women, they patted her shoulder as they let out their ululations and wails. His sister, the widow, who had walked the same path for her husband a month earlier and was not yet twenty-five years old, held a picture of her brother in one hand and her baby in the other. She walked with a firm, deliberate tread beside her younger sister. The family had congregated among the people behind the bier of the oldest brother and, upon finding themselves lost to each other within the crowd, began turning around in fear—Ali too. For an instant he forgot he was watching his brother's coffin, he utterly forgot his surroundings. He forgot his brother's face and the weeping eyes all around him. He remembered that one of Zayn's men had shouted at a woman who was wailing and ordered her to perform ululations instead because the soldier's funeral was his wedding to the homeland. Ali caught sight of the woman as she gave the man a fearful look, then watched as she reformed portions of her face. She wiped her tears and obediently let out ululations without cease, while Ali's mother let out a scream: "Where did you go when you left me, waghaly, my darling boy?"

Ali remembered walking behind the bier, the

village sheikh taking hold of his hand and gently pulling him along; then they went into the graveyard and saw the hole. So it hadn't been a dream after all. The same shape, the same layers of soil, the same pink worms. They were lowering the coffin, and everywhere there were oak and sycamore trees, and the graveyard was enclosed by stone walls that had been laid with care. All around he could see numerous holes that the village had filled; when they buried his sister's husband a month earlier, the ground hadn't been dug up like this. He saw the hole intended for his brother and knew once again that he wasn't dead. A woman with red hair appeared between the men, and he recalled that he knew her, but nothing more than that. Her face was vague, though her dishevelled red hair and her long dress conveyed something to him. She was trying to slip past Zayn, whom Ali had never dreamed of seeing or speaking to, yet here he was, right in front of him, accompanied by men who carried rifles even though they weren't soldiers. They fired a succession of salvos at the sky when they reached the burial ground, and Ali shuddered. All this had been a year ago maybe; he couldn't really remember anymore. He knew they had come back from their daily work in the plains, Ali and his father, when they found the house in an uproar of weeping and had learned, along with some other things that would cause his head to ache, that his brother no longer existed, while their two-room house turned into a salon for the throngs of neighbours arriving from all over. They brought food and drink, they wailed and lamented, and each of them related a story about a son they had lost, as his mother gazed around blankly. During the burial, Ali kept his eyes turned in her direction. She kept trying to push forward through the men to reach the coffin but couldn't. When the woman with red hair appeared, one of Zayn's men grabbed her and flung her out of the group of men lined up around the grave, as his father stroked the coffin. It was draped in the country's flag, a beautiful, gleaming flag edged with golden embroidery that his father's fingers traced as his mother tried to forge a path forward and a woman said to her "Weep, Nahla, weep!" His mother's name was Nahla, then—now he remembered! And Nahla, whose name he recalled as he lay beneath the afternoon sun, wasn't weeping. Then the woman with the red hair fell down, and he turned to her, and he remembered who she was.

On his back on the ground facing the tree, he realised she was Humayrouna. He contracted his body among the leaves and heard a rustling. He saw the entire hole, proving he wasn't dead, and saw that Humayrouna, when she approached the grave, was trying to touch the coffin to bid farewell as she had sworn to the villagers she would do whenever their young men were consigned to the soil. And every time, they would drag her away from the graveyard, heaping abuse on her and telling her not to go near the men as they were burying their dead. "Oh, so that's how it is! We can't go near men when they're burying men ... Aha!"

She spat on the ground and repeated that same phrase. Humayrouna didn't care that she'd been turned away, she simply circled round the crowd and slipped back in among them. She grabbed the mother's thobe and pulled her along, evading the arms of the surrounding women. The ranks of men were solid, pressed tightly together as they listened to the sheikh recite the Fatiha over the soul of the fallen. Ali's brother was a son of their village, although they hadn't known him very well; a few knew the dead boy because he had worked as a hired labourer on their lands before he'd volunteered for the army. But the duty of being out in his funeral procession in this cold, rainy weather was unavoidable; they were all labouring under a single misfortune, and sooner or later they would lose their own sons in turn. Some of them vaguely recalled that the martyr and his family came from that group of people who were invisible. They were hired labour, and if it wasn't for the portions of meat they distributed on religious holidays to the poor of the village, the villagers would never even consider stopping to greet them. Now, all the villagers were in the graveyard, waiting for their duty to come to an end so they could go back to thinking about how they would feed whichever of their children were left. They had no time to listen to the senile old woman they called, with slight contempt, "Humayrouna," for her red hair. When one of them, raising a portrait of the Leader, screamed that the martyr had died for the President, someone else yelled back that he had died for the nation, and the sheikh said, "Praise God for all things, in the presence of death there is no call for all this, ya shabab ... May God have mercy on his soul." Next to him was the new sheikh, one of Zayn's men. They didn't respect him like they did the old sheikh, but they feared him. So as soon as the old sheikh spoke, Zayn's new sheikh barged forwards and shouted, "We are all loyal to the President *and* the nation!" Then an armed man approached the sheikh and whispered something in his ear so that his face paled, and a shot rang out, and the Kalashnikov rifles rose towards the sky, and the villagers trembled, and the women ululated, and the crowd seemed to be swaying in an undulating motion in time with the bullets. The women shouted the names of their martyred sons and asked the martyr's brother to convey their greetings and love to their children in the other world. The names began to be repeated here and there, flying with their sighs, and with each name the gunfire resumed. During all the commotion, Ali's mother and Humayrouna sneaked between the men while the men fixed their eyes on the sky as it received the scattered bullets, and the young men shouted in quavering voices, "Zaffo al-shaheed ... today is the martyr's wedding, zaffo ... zaffo!" The women ululated, and a man yelled it was time for them to bid goodbye to the Earth's gift that had been given in trust. But by this time Nahla had reached the coffin and was screaming "I want to see my son, I want to smell him!" The crowd was taken by surprise. Nahla was lying on top of the coffin and embracing it tightly. The rain had stopped, and the mother's body appeared nailed in place. There was no force capable of tearing her away. The flag slid into the hole and she clung to the wood as she tried to prise the coffin open. The men sprang forward to pull her away, but she dodged them. Then Ali saw Nahla. He was looking at her, offering no help to his father or the other men in plucking her off the coffin. Was that the scene? Yes, it was definitely his brother's funeral, he remembered Nahla fell into the grave along with the coffin—a disgrace to herself and in defiance of the traditions that barred women from approaching the graveside with the men. She fell first, then the coffin fell on top of her. It was nailed shut and she couldn't open it. Silence descended for a moment, and it seemed as though Nahla had buried herself. There wasn't a single sound from her, not a rattle of the throat, not a moan. She could hear a clamour, and feared that her bones would break beneath the weight of the coffin. When she opened her eyes, she saw men's hands reaching down to take the coffin out of the hole again. Ali watched her, goggle-eyed, and didn't move forward to help. He just stood there thunderstruck, watching the men as they tried to pull his mother out of the grave. At last she had succeeded in saying goodbye to her son, even though she'd only smelled soil while listening to abuse from men who only cared about the fact that a woman had disrespected the laws of their religion and the hurma of the dead. Humayrouna cursed them and told them they were trash, that they had to let this poor woman say goodbye to her son. When Zayn told the red-haired old woman to shut up and get out of the graveyard, she roared back, "Get out yourself, wijh nahas!" Then she spat in his face. One of Zayn's men rebuked her and drove her away with the end of his gun. She wasn't strong enough to bear anything more than that. She fell next to the grave and saw Nahla's fingers welded around the coffin.

Ali took hold of his mother after the men raised her up, and everyone left. At first she was leaning against him, but she soon fell over, so he picked her up with one arm and didn't turn around, ignoring the comments of the people around him. Humayrouna stumbled and spluttered behind them, leaning on her cane. Nahla was white as a ghost, her clothes were soaked with mud, and her hands were trembling. The men and women had forgotten her existence in their own grief for the young man who had died, but suddenly one of the women happened to notice Ali as he was carrying his mother away; the woman howled and shouted her name, and the crowd turned to watch Ali and his mother leave the funeral. The two of them incurred everyone's wrath that day, and they couldn't withstand it. The people shouted at him to come back. Then Ali, carrying his mother on one arm, stopped and shouted a curse on them, and on their fathers and mothers. For the first time in his life, Ali could touch his mother's cheeks, which were chapped, either by cold or sunshine, he wasn't exactly sure. He only knew that the roughness of that red, riven skin, the dead flakes clinging to his mother's face like jutting thorns, had allowed him, finally, to hear the rattle in his throat as he stared dry-eyed into the sky.

Chapter 3

Behind the tree, beneath the scorching sun, he could see someone opposite him on the other side of the trunk … A living being, a chimera formed by the cruelty of the silence, perhaps, or an enemy flung there by the bomb, just as the bomb had sent him and his comrades flying.

Rust? Or was it the taste of fear? A rusty-tasting fear he had experienced recently. The taste of rust was nothing more than the smell of explosions, and look how easily he swallowed it down. His heart was pounding. He raised his head as he watched the head opposite him. The other head was doing the same thing. He gulped down a deep breath and closed his eyes.

In the middle of the sky, he imagined how he and the Other looked; two men shaking off branches, leaves, mud, and soil, lifting their heads to watch each other while in the distance the horizon of the sea appeared infinite. He was used to tracing pictures like this—closing his eyes and imagining that he was seeing things from above. He had been born on a high mountain peak and was used to observing things that lay far below him; when he climbed the tree by their house, there was nothing above him but sky. From there he would imagine how his mother might appear from above; or how his tree would look, his arzal, the village paths, Humayrouna, the mountain ridges when they met in their ravines. Right now he could imagine the scene: a living thing, moving, observing him and imitating his movements. It seemed like an exact double of him. And there were no birds in the sky! Odd that the birds had disappeared on such a sunny summer's day. As for the mountains, which bloodshed and war had passed over for thousands of years, they calmly reclined to the sea, confident that all this was nothing more than a temporary scuffle. They wouldn't be shaken by the bomb that fell by mistake when a plane dropped its load on the patrol stationed on the summit.

Ali didn't understand why the plane had dropped that bomb. How could the plane drop a bomb when it was supposed to be protecting them? How had they made such a mistake? He couldn't move. All his surroundings were blurry and confused. He thought he must have been wounded, though he couldn't see where his wound was, and he was alone, the other soldiers were all dead, burned up. Whichever way they'd died, he couldn't see a single one of them now, couldn't even hear a groan.

So. He was alone. And this tree, which he knew by heart, just as he had memorised the topography of the trees in his village, seemed like the twin of his tree next to the maqam. Light broke in his heart—he considered the resemblance a good omen! The tree would protect him, he knew—just as they protected the maqams and everyone who sought refuge there.

As soon as he could raise his upper body and lean on his right elbow, he shouted in pain and fell back, then he noticed the head opposite him had also risen, shouted, then slid back, just like his own. The echo of their cries resounded among the mountains. The movements of this Other confused him. It occurred to Ali that he was seeing his shadow, or observing a similar world parallel to this one. Perhaps it was the sun's glare that made it appear ... or maybe he really was over there. The silhouettes of the movement he kept repeating could be seen from the other side, and he thought he saw himself being mocked by the movements of the Other, or his shadow, or his hallucination, whatever it was. He was no longer sure of anything, except the fact he was waiting for someone to come and rescue him. Perhaps it had not yet been very long; perhaps this wait, which seemed like more than a century to Ali, had in fact only been a few hours. When had the bomb fallen? He couldn't remember. Little by little he had regained his head and his trees—his tree here where he was lying, and his tree there, back in the village. And he knew that woman, too; her image was becoming so clear he could make out her eyes, steeped in time. He could even see their colour: white-grey, like the eyes of the blind. She wasn't entirely blind herself, however. She would point a trembling finger and say to him, "Here it is, in my head; I see in my head, not with my eyes." She was the one who told him that the maqam's tree was her only friend and that she was looking after him because he was her friend's son. In the village, they used to shout at her to stop spouting nonsense to Ali because the boy was mad enough already, and she would spit on them.

He recognised himself again. He recalled Humayrouna, who told him the story of the trees. He had to focus, he didn't have much time—it had already taken half a day for him just to wake up and move his body, to realise he was alive, who he was, what his name was, and to remember his mother and her name. And now he knew Humayrouna too. Divine providence was following him, otherwise this old woman would never have occurred to him. This woman, who had raised him and taught him the language of trees, used to say that—contrary to the lies that were told—it was the trees which maintained the earth's solidity, by pushing deep into its core. The villagers used to mock this woman, who was over a hundred years old and still dyed her hair with red henna which over the years had turned a gaudy orange. For the last thirty years she had asked one of the women to help her with it. The choice was made at random; she would knock at a door and call a woman by name, ordering her to come outside to henna her hair. It seemed ridiculous to the villagers, but to Humayrouna, it was a matter of life or death—she hated white hair. She often said as much to Ali, and would spit on the passage of time. She lived at the base of the tree, but this didn't stop her from keeping herself, her hair, and her peculiar clothing clean. She wore a long gown closed by a colourful belt, and on her head was placed an embroidered scarf, delicately crocheted in wheat-coloured silken threads, which she used to say was as old as she was. She would wrap it around her face on cold days so that nothing was visible bar her eyes, and she guarded it like her own life. Humayrouna used to tell Ali many things. Before he joined the army she told him she knew the year was 2013, and that she had been born a hundred years earlier. She would live longer than she should, but if she did happen to die, then she would be anyway content; having already lived a century, she had been able to rile an inordinate number of "scum," as she called them. One day, as they were sitting under the maqam's tree, she asked Ali if he had ever fallen in love; he didn't respond, or blush, or react any way at all. He just stared into space and felt a deep pain such as he had never before experienced. As for Humayrouna, she yelled loudly in her thick dialect, "You know, Ali, anyone who doesn't know love, doesn't know life, see!" Then, trembling, she stood up and stammered on. "Look at me ... What am I? Turkish, French, Arab ... I knew them all ... I have known love, and my heart will die at peace ... Look at these mountains. I know all of them, and on every mountain there is a story of mine ... Ah, time—" Just then, before she had finished what she was saying, a man coming out of the maqam flung a curse at her, demanding that she remember her grey hair. She ignored him, and resumed her phrase sorrowfully, "Ah, time!" Then she laughed. Pointing at the mountain peak facing them, she went on: "There ... there ... where people like you, all of you, can't bear life's cruelty. There, *I lived*." She said all this in the most refined Arabic. Ali was not surprised that their home was on the mountaintop, and he didn't believe there was any peak higher. Humayrouna kept laughing in her shrill, persistent way, ending with gasps and tears rolling over her cheeks as she said, "Allah, deliver us from laughter! I've seen people grow afraid if they hear laughter ... You see, we're afraid even to laugh here!" Then she laughed again.

For the first two days after Ali was born, he was breathing but didn't let out a single cry. Everyone thought he would die. Humayrouna used to look after families like Ali's. Usually this solicitude of hers was nothing more than the occasional visit, but when she heard that Nahla had birthed a weakling baby boy, she hurried over, tottering on her cane. She entered the house without knocking and informed the terrified Nahla that her son would live. Then she shouted at everyone present that they'd stifle the baby by gathering together in here like this: "This room is as cramped as a scorpion's cunt. We want him to breathe!" She commanded Nahla to pick up the baby and follow her to the maqam.

The villagers said she was crazy, but experience had taught successive generations to heed this woman who came out with strange advice. No one knew where she had picked any of it up. She could read, but had stopped ten years earlier when her eyesight grew too bad. She would sing in a strange language; Ali heard some people saying it was Syriac, and others that she had learned Turkish, because she had lived among the Turks after her father was lost in the Seferberlik. She knew French as well, because she used to work as a nurse alongside the French forces. She had even accompanied one of their engineers as he planned the construction of bridges in these remote mountain areas, and she had stayed with a delegation from the French Mandate government, dispatched to construct a school in one of the mountain villages. It was at this school she learned to read and write. One person declared that she had attended one of General Gouraud's receptions, and others affirmed that she used to meet Sheikh Saleh Ali and his men. Myriad legends were told about her and no one knew the truth, although it was generally believed that she came from the distant northern mountains, when Iskenderun was still part of Syria. Humayrouna herself got mixed up, as she could no longer remember much about her early life, apart from the fact she had been born on the day war broke out; one of the many wars that humans are so busy inventing. She had remained hale thanks to her memory, so she always said, although the stories she told about herself were a source of doubt for many. She grew frightened when they teased her that she and death were close friends.

Nineteen years ago, when Ali was born, she was still part of their daily lives and they paid attention to what she said. So Nahla hurried, although she could only walk after Humayrouna slowly, not because she was tired, but because, as her life had become more prolonged, she had acquired a limp and a habit of listing to one side, so much so that an onlooker might imagine she was about to topple over with every step. Humayrouna stayed in the maqam with Nahla, both women rubbing Ali's body with oil that had been blessed. Humayrouna ordered Nahla to put the baby next to the maqam's tree, which forked out into several large branches forming a square large enough to cover four people seated. She put Ali in this square, lit some incense over the nearest branch, and stayed there next to him, muttering. The tree shaded the maqam, like every maqam that lay over the plains and the mountains all the way to the sea. Every maqam lay in the shadow of trees that were hundreds of years old, and because they were sacred, unmolested by human hand.

That tree—which years later in the war would become a shelter for the village's widows when a site known as the "Widow's Quarter" would be established next to it—that tree was where Ali let out his first cry. His mother, father, and brothers gathered around him and murmured, and they prayed that God would save him. At night, the village doctor came and told them that the newborn was in good health, and they should go home.

Over the following years the villagers would tell Ali that Humayrouna had saved his life. She told them that Ali was the son of the tree, and that a new life had been written for him. As for Humayrouna, after Ali grew up and started going to the village school, she begged him not to have his head turned by those idiots. She said that when he was a baby she had done what she did to bring him out of that cramped den, that so-called house. But that wherever he went, he was the son of the tree. With each year that passed she would tell him stories that came from up and down and all over the mountains. She used to visit the family in the morning and stay until the afternoon, and whenever Nahla grumbled at her, she would retort, "What? Did you forget that I have a share in him just as much as you do?" And Nahla would fall silent and allow her to stay. When Ali was four, Humayrouna started bringing him with her to the maqam. As for Ali, aside from the roof of their house, which overhung the mountain, and his arzal, the outer tree branches were his refuge. He would learn to fly among the branches until he was able to move between the trees with delicate bounds. The villagers used to see him flying among the trees in the forest, weaving skilfully in and out of the leaves. Later on, he was content to live between the maqam's tree and his arzal's tree, flying between their branches. Those around him would discover that he rarely spoke. He could converse with the birds, however, and the village kids gave him a nickname: Humayrouna's blackbird.

The village stood around a small open square; its houses lay on the steps of the mountain, and in the middle there was a small cluster of cramped, shabby houses. Humayrouna often inspected them, passing by each one in turn, but she only ate in the maqam's courtyard. This rule everyone knew: there was always a meal waiting there for her, provided by the villagers. Later on, during the war, while they were drowning in their grief and their suffering and their hunger, they would forget her for a while, only to remember her all of sudden. Fortunately for her, the villagers used to visit the maqam to offer up sacrifices that they hoped would protect their sons on the frontlines, and Humayrouna had priority over these offerings at the maqam. She always called herself the maqam's guardian. The men weren't concerned by the word of a woman like her—she was cheerful and chatty, and no one saw her as anything other than a dog in need of food. It was the only reason they put up with everything she said. But during their religious meetings they would turn her out and wouldn't allow her near the maqam. In recent years the new sheikh had got into the habit of cursing her and chasing her away without anyone daring to stop him—in fact, there were many who followed his example.

No one knew Humayrouna's real name, and she claimed to have forgotten it herself. It was rumoured that her real name was Yamama. Ali was sitting in her lap once when she spat in a man's face after he called her "Yamama." She retorted that Yamama was dead. He asked her, "What *is* your name?" And she replied, "I'm the tree's sister, dummy, and Ali's her son!"

Ali remembered how she used to live at the bottom of the tree trunk, on the side where the sun went down. She used to claim it was the best place in the world to live because she went to sleep with the sun. She would shut the door that faced the sun and close her eyes, and as soon as the sun set in the sea she would disappear along with her piled-up odds and ends. People never saw her after the sun vanished. When a particularly spiteful woman asked why she dyed her hair orange, Humayrouna retorted, "It's sun colour ... the sun gives me this colour!" She built her small shack right underneath the tree. Back then she had been in her fifties and could rely on the help of whoever happened to be around. She informed the villagers she was going to become the servant of the maqam; this was forbidden for women, but they agreed she should stay and protect it because she told them she had no family. Her *barrakiyya*, as she called it, was a shack of wood and sheet tin, composed of a single room where all her mysterious bits and pieces were crammed. No one knew what was inside apart from Ali. In the rock at the base of the tree she had carved herself a hole for a chair and covered it with cushions, and there was also an old stone basin where she soaked fruit and vegetables, and washed her clothes. She was permitted to walk through the orchards and pick pears, apples, and peaches, whatever she wanted, without payment or supervision. Her greatest pleasure lay in making cigarettes from balady tobacco. Despite the tremors and the weakness in her fingers, she was still able to roll a cigarette like a true craftsman. The farmers would give her tobacco leaves for free and she would grind it herself. She would take a leaf, unroll it under the eyes of the young Ali, and chop it into two pieces. Then she would sniff them and cry, "Allah Allah! Oh for the days of Abu Riha balady." And then she would tell him the story of Abu Riha tobacco, and many other stories too. She taught him that the scent of Abu Riha smoke was the smell of oppression, a familiar perfume to the poor who lived on these mountains two hundred years ago. She explained how, back then, the farmers took up arms against the Turks because of the taxes that had been imposed on them, and the feudal families from the mountain villages collaborated with the Turks. The farmers couldn't sell their crops, which lay abandoned for an entire year in their houses, a year in which they died of starvation. These houses had one single room for the farmers for sleeping, eating and drinking, and raising their livestock in, and it was here they hung the strings of tobacco, lit the fire in the stove, and had their children—all in the same room. She told Ali that this tobacco was a rare type because the leaves stored the smell of people after having inhaled the perfume of their lives for an entire year. After that year, the farmers managed to sell their harvest to Egyptian traders through middlemen who were drawn from the mountain villages and from the large feudal families of the area. She said to Ali that back then people still had dignity. The rich families grew richer, and the farmers who sold their smell and their subjection grew poorer. Nevertheless, poverty didn't stop the farmers from becoming accustomed to producing that same kind of tobacco over the following years after the Egyptians deemed it excellent, and it became known as Lattakian tobacco. She told him that she had worked in the Régie Company before the state nationalised it, and she could distinguish different types of tobacco with her nose alone. She used to laugh as she narrated stories to Ali, who heard many of them from her. She said she would tell him her true story at some point, when he was a man; she promised.

Over the last five years they had stopped her from cleaning the maqam. Before that she had been allowed to do it under the supervision of the maqam's servant. Decades earlier, the man serving the maqam had been a Sufi ascetic. Those were foggy days no one now remembered; they had been prepared to forget things as life went on, but lost only life's sweetness – its bitterness remained lodged in their memories. This Sufi was one of the sheikhs who spent their days reading, writing, and teaching the fundamentals of language, religion, and poetry. These men had spiritual and social authority over their sect, but then a new class of sheikhs emerged in the eighties, just as the power of the President the Father was being consolidated. Humayrouna wouldn't go near any of these newcomers. She took her knowledge from the old sheikhs who were beginning to pass away. She learned from them, listened to them and followed their teachings, and nobody noticed this woman with red hair who called herself by strange names at night. She committed everything they said to memory, and day by day she was able to repeat yet more lines of poetry by august men of religion, by princes, and by saints. She even memorised the Qur'an and chanted it in the mornings, and the villagers enjoyed hearing her cheerful, melodious voice. From her, Ali learned poetry, and the Qur'an, and the sounds of the trees and the birds. He was diligent in his almost daily visits to her, kindling resentment in Nahla, especially when the villagers kept saying that Humayrouna had passed on her madness to Ali. Humayrouna would look at him proudly and say, "This one is going to be a man of religion and truth." Over time Ali's furious mother forgot her bitterness, absorbed as she was in her daily labour on the lands of others.

Now Ali raised his hand, leaned on it, then rose up a little way so he could see where he was wounded. His right upper thigh was split deep into the flesh and a long wound had opened up inside the ripped fabric, but summoning up his memories of Humayrouna had helped the muscles in his face relax. As he passed his fingers along the edges of the deep wound, the stickiness of his blood burned him and he was sure that what he had seen when he first gained consciousness was nothing more than the phantoms of his older brother's funeral in the graveyard. That day had been the first time in a long time that Humayrouna had appeared. She was agitated and upset, looking anxiously between him and the coffin. She stood next to him and stuttered quietly, "Maybe it's time for you to leave the village, my heart." Then she grabbed his mother's hand, and pulled her so they could sneak forward between the men. As Ali shifted his wounded leg, he remembered that she spat in Zayn's face that day. He happened to turn in the direction of the sun, where his double was moving. It was also looking at the sun, leaning on its right elbow, just like Ali. He had forgotten the Other until then. He wanted to know the distance between the sun and the opposite mountain peak, so he could estimate how much daylight was left.

Chapter 4

The ball fell.

He remembered where the pain in his head had been, and how his face was smeared with dust as he was toppled by the blow that landed in the very same place that was hurting now. What a difference there was between those two extremes of pain. But he saw it, saw the football spinning quickly, disappearing in its circle, then reappearing and falling on his head.

Ali wasn't trying to move at this point. The phantom of the ball that had caused him to fall into a black hole was confusing him again; nevertheless, he was glad to feel his cheek pressing against the earth and he could feel the roots that appeared above ground like undulating snakes, and he caught their familiar smell. He was stuck somewhere between life and death, or between death and life—was there such an enormous difference between these two designations? He couldn't think of any; he didn't like language anyway, he preferred floating around in his own world. Then he heard the shout, it tore him in half like a razorblade and brought a weak moan with it. His forehead wrinkled, and the world around him disappeared as he sank into a fit of agony. Sounds came back, emerging from his head, and he heard the same scream and the ball was spinning and spinning: "Yaa, huu, hey people, the President is dead, everyone! Our President is dead, you godforsaken lot! Yaa, huu, hey people! Everyone!" The phrase was shouted in his ear with renewed urgency.

Who said that phrase? *Yaa, huu, ya nas, ya alim, the President is dead.* It came to him now. He was in a state of unbalance. He was surrounded by all kinds of feelings, hanging in the air, burning in the fire, falling into a deep hole, and seeing the ball that swooped and fell in the small schoolyard. Ali had been at school on that day of fear. He remembered the blow he received from the owner of the shop attached to the school. That shopkeeper had hit him with the ball, then proceeded to rain blows on everyone else as well. That dark, skinny man with bulging cheeks was able to make his wife swell up every nine months so she was permanently inflated, standing next to her husband in the shop, carrying and emptying cardboard boxes. As for the little ones, who kept multiplying, they were like a miraculous series of skinny, emaciated creatures leaping round her, and Ali liked to compare them to brown worms. The shopkeeper was proud of his children, who built small rooms of their own when they grew up, in which they generated more children (or worms) that spread all over the mountains. Despite being fifty years old the shopkeeper insisted on calling himself "Slick." Ali knew this word meant the shopkeeper was smart, and he didn't laugh or wonder why the man called himself that. He also knew he received a terrible punch after shooting the ball, the ball that danced in front of his eyes as he was trying to reach the tree. "Yaa, huu, ya nas, ya alim, the President is dead, lock yourselves up in your houses. Wallahi, may we all die ourselves!" All the children screamed, apart from Ali. There were more than ten of them in the schoolyard, which they had entered through a circular hole in the wall, large enough for their small bodies to squeeze through. The primary school was situated in the centre of the village, and the schoolyard was the only flat space where the boys could gather and play football. Ali wasn't one of those who adored football, but he followed his older brother there. Perhaps he was six or seven at that time; he had mastered reading and writing, and he still went frequently to the maqam to listen to the elderly sheikh and the poetry that Humayrouna would repeat for him. On that day in June, Ali's father had yelled at him to get down from the roof and help shift the stone for repairing the wall that had collapsed in the snow earlier that year. Ali leapt up to escape, following his brother who had gone to the schoolyard to record the goals. This was how boys became men, by recording goals—that was what his brother told him. So Ali joined his brother, not thinking the match would end with a beating at the hands of Slick, who hopped and leapt and hit the children as he shouted that the President was dead.

In front of him Ali saw the ball with the strange black-and-white squares. (He would learn, later on, that they weren't really squares, according to the engineering his younger brother was so talented at.) Ali would be enchanted by the ball he loved, because before long he saw it could fly, swooping between legs, returning to other legs, playing with the ground and the air. Maybe, like him, it liked playing with the wind. "Shoot!" his brother said, and raised his hand up high. So Ali shot, and his heart leapt. There was a moment when Ali was still in the air, watching the speed of the ball he had launched, and the ball was flying, and the boys were looking at it in amazement, and it cleared the school wall and landed somewhere, and Ali's older brother looked at him proudly, and Ali's chest swelled. The boys were angry—their ball was lost—and it became evident that Ali's powerful shot had landed on the head of the shopkeeper, who burst out crying and accosted them through the hole in the school wall, bending over and shouting, "Ya wlad, sixty dogs are out here playing while our President is dead. Go on, yalla, see for yourselves. Go home and lock yourselves in. The President is dead, people ... wallahi, if only you lot would die instead!" The open-mouthed boys came closer to him. They had never seen a grown man cry and leap about before, striking his face like the women did, and they saw the snot that streamed endlessly. Ali drew closer with the others, then he looked at the blue sky, seeing how the shopkeeper raised his hands towards it beseechingly, "Ya rab ... ya rab, have mercy on us, Lord!" The boys looked at each other in fear and bewilderment. Ali couldn't see whatever it was in the sky that the shopkeeper was so frightened of, and his heart trembled because by that point the boys had started crying too, and the shopkeeper was cursing them, and their mothers were cursing and slapping them in turn. The blow Ali received had knocked him to the ground, and the blows that followed on the others made them all fall silent. They didn't understand what they were supposed to do, when the shopkeeper's howling resumed: "Yalla, go home, lock yourselves up and cry for a thousand years. Wallahi, may we be miserable forever!" One boy piped up and shouted at the shopkeeper to leave them alone, before the man's oldest daughter-in-law appeared, pulling her hair and howling at them to stop playing out of respect for the departed—who, it turned out, hadn't been immortal after all. The boys clustered around the ball which had been flung at their feet and the shopkeeper spat on it. Each one of the children bore the marks of blows on their face or head and were crying from pain and shock, all apart from Ali; he was on the verge of charging at the shopkeeper when the other boys stopped him. They left the locked-up school and the schoolyard and jumped through the wall, and looked nonplussed at the narrow street and then the shopkeeper, who resumed yelling at them: "Yalla, shut yourselves up at home. Get going!" They looked at the picture hanging on the wall, and on the wall of the shopkeeper's house that joined onto the shop. There were many pictures of the President hanging all around, and the boys realised that something very serious had happened. These pictures had been hanging there for so long they had forgotten them. There weren't only pictures of the President, but also a statue of him in the town; they used to find him everywhere. By now, the boys were looking at each other in alarm. They knew they should run home, because the man whose face had been part of their lives since they were born, the man who had been present everywhere, was now dead. The man and his pictures were on their schoolbooks, on every wall inside their school building, on the television screen, the walls of their homes, the headteacher's office, on the classroom wall, on the blackboard. This man was dead. Ali's older brother said to him, "Ya wilaah ... turns out Presidents can die. I honestly didn't think they could ... turns out they die, just like everyone else!" The children ran home along the village pathways, all slipping onto different paths. Ali and his brother ran so quickly that their heels hit their backsides. They were obliged to run further than the other children as their house lay at the far end of the village. They saw people behaving strangely, saw women emerge from their houses wailing, but when Ali turned towards the maqam and saw the oak, it was standing as it always had. Uneasy, he considered leaving his brother and going into the maqam and seeing what Humayrouna was doing. Then he wondered if the earth was going to split open and swallow them all up, just as his schoolteacher had told them. It was a phrase he heard often: "Inshallah, the earth will split open and swallow you up and rid me of you all." He didn't understand this at the time, but Humayrouna told him that the earth really had split open and swallowed people and that the underneath sometimes flipped over to become the top in these plains by the sea—time and time again it flipped over, and they called this constant turmoil *earthquakes*. When he grew older he learned that the earth was the one to flip, not the people. He didn't understand why the teacher used to pray for the earth to split open and swallow them up, but as he was running home with his brother he heard that same phrase again, from an old woman: "If only the earth had split open and swallowed me before this day came." Ali pictured the earth as a large cooking pot they were all falling inside, and imagined a giant, tyrannical being called The President looming over them, putting the lid on, and boiling them alive inside. Or perhaps The President was the giant that would protect them when the earth split open and the beasts came to swallow them up. He told himself this as he ran, not shedding a single tear all the while. His brother was crying and Ali was observing people running and weeping. Ali's brother took his hand and pulled him close, saying "Don't be scared" while his tears gushed. Ali gritted his teeth and bit his lips, and sweat streamed from his forehead. He ran and ran until his cotton T-shirt was soaked. Seven-year-old Ali was good at two things: whistling and being alone—being alone was what he was best at. It seemed stupid to others, but he knew – and had done for the entirety of his short life – that he wanted exactly this: to be alone with his tree, letting his vast and unconfined world bloom, a world unknown to others. He couldn't catch up to his brother, who grabbed his hand and dragged Ali along behind him. Ali felt like he couldn't breathe properly. His brother was running and Ali had to follow him; if not, he would face the pomegranate cane. His father's cane was long and thin, and it let out a hissing noise with every movement. His brother looked at him, shouting, "Hurry up, jackass." Here, his older brother noticed that Ali was still carrying the football, clutching it at his chest and pressing it to his heart. Panicked, his older brother stopped and cuffed him. Ali fell down but he still didn't cry; he merely hugged the ball tighter. His brother grabbed his hand and they ran so fast that their heels slapped their backsides again, until it seemed like they were flying. When they reached the house Ali climbed the wooden stairs to the roof and heard the neighbours calling from a distance, "Come outside, wakhiti, come out, sister. Wallahi, our time has come!" His mother came outside in tears and went into the woman's house with her children and shut the door. They forgot about Ali, on the roof, hugging the ball. Then he saw the neighbours, far and near, creeping around furtively and disappearing, locking their windows. Ali heard their laments and howls, and he stroked the surface of the ball. Perhaps they would come looking for it, but he felt reassured that the boys and their families were preoccupied with the death of the President they had thought would never die. Ali was waiting on the rooftop in front of the mountain, watching the slope and the houses, waiting for the earth to split open and swallow them all up as his teacher had said. He reflected that his teacher had actually said something else: that he would beat them and beat them until the earth split open and swallowed them—and that had nothing to do with the death of the President. Thirteen years later he would recall that the earth had remained as it was that day, it hadn't split open and swallowed them up while he was sitting on the flat roof with his ball, watching the sun and the forest at the foot of the mountain slope. He'd stood up then and made his way to the edge of the roof overlooking the slope. He'd carefully placed the ball on the ground, retreated a few steps, and stared at the few clouds in the sky. Then he'd shot the ball in the air and watched as it flew up high, hovered and fell, vanishing into the valley. After that, he turned around and caught sight of the branches of the oak tree at the maqam. Some people were gathered there but he couldn't make out who; the tree branches were in the way, and he was too far away to tell them apart. He went to the edge of the roof and spread his arms, imagining the motion of the ball as it tumbled into the wadi. He had a half-formed thought of flying after it when suddenly he heard a shout from his mother, who was waving at him to join the others. Forgetting he was barefoot, he left his plastic slippers on the roof and ran without stopping until he reached the place where they were all gathering. He couldn't see Humayrouna anywhere. He heard weeping and wailing, and he slipped in among the throng. He saw terrified faces, and words were flying about. "Trust in God, everyone," said the old sheikh, while the new sheikh gathered some young men around him and spoke to them in a whisper. Ali was able to slip into the maqam and he saw Humayrouna at last, sitting in the zawiya. All around her, women and men were lighting incense and muttering, and he spotted the picture where the virtuous saints were gathered, the President among them. No one knew who had hung the picture there. Then he saw a woman carrying a picture of the President and wallowing in tears, so he crammed himself in between Humayrouna's feet. The old woman seemed dazed and only half-conscious as she uneasily watched everything going on around her. Ali got closer to her and looked in her eyes. He saw a white void; she wasn't looking at him. She took him in her arms like she usually did, but she didn't utter a syllable, staring entreatingly at the last green circle in the hollow of the maqam's dome. As for the shopkeeper, he was still screaming, "Ya wilkun ... God curse all of your fathers... our President is dead!" The days that followed, filled with silence and foreboding, weighed heavily on the villagers. Eventually Ali stopped hearing the howls. He had fled to his woods and climbed down the wadi, thinking about his football. He disappeared during the day and slept on the roof of the house at night. Before too long, perhaps after a month, joy returned to people's souls. Shouting rose again on the village paths. The shopkeeper continued yelling, but now they were cries of delight or exultation. After that month had passed, Ali saw the shopkeeper bounding around once again, hopping and skipping, shouting and screaming, making rounds of the houses, whipping up his daughters-in-law and his grandchildren and all the villagers, urging them to start ululating, windmilling his hands: "Long live the President ... Long live the President!" When Ali wondered how the President had died then come alive again, he thought for an instant that he must be immortal after all. He hadn't yet learned that this new President was the son of that other President, and that this phrase which he found so peculiar—the President is dead, long live the President—wasn't as strange as he had thought. The son of the President had become the new President, and commander of the armed forces, and secretary general of the party that his father had bequeathed him.

Ali hadn't known any of this. He was confused as he observed the shopkeeper and his funny movements—how he had laughed that day! Ali soon forgot all about the shopkeeper, how he lived in prosperity and contentment from that day on, and only came to remember him during the war when he spotted the shopkeeper walking in his children's funeral processions. The man seemed like a withered old tree.

Now a deep headache washed over Ali as he watched a phantom of the ball spin in front of him then disappear. As he launched it, his attention was caught by a passing cloud, and he thought that the football which vanished into the valley was no rival for the clouds as they climbed and vanished in the sky. He was struck by the bitterness of the fall, which he himself was experiencing now with his weakness and his wounds. He believed that his past and present life consisted of nothing more than the few metres between the place where the bomb landed and the trunk of the tree. A short, complete life—enough. And when he felt this short distance was all the life he had left, he asked himself what he was doing here. Who was he fighting, and on whose behalf? Who was he? It was the first time he had considered this question: Who was he really, and who did he used to be? Were the few metres that separated him from the tree trunk the summation of his life? Was it a life he had lived, or a brief, fleeting passage? Would he be a star in the sky? He recalled the face of his brother, who had been destined to fight in defence of the state on the very front lines, but he couldn't find any answers to his questions, which arrived in a torrent: What alien life could he see? Was it the life of another being? As if he were seeing some other nineteen-year-old man tossed onto a mountain peak and bombed by mistake, as if he were trying to understand what this young man was doing in the few metres left of his life, in choosing to remain alive.

He shifted his ribs, stretched, and opened his eyes to make sure he was still alive, still within this lifespan measured in metres, and as he did so he saw the phantom of the football flying. He let out a sigh and fell into a ravine of questions and torment. Isolated from himself in that moment, his thoughts wandered to his double. He wanted to know just one thing: whether he could turn his face now, overcoming the pain in his head, which reminded him of the blow from the football. He wanted to know if that Other would raise his head too. His apprehensions would be eliminated in an instant if that Other was his soul, waiting for him.

Chapter 5

No sooner had his mind cleared again than the strange heaviness at the base of his head overwhelmed him and pushed him back until he lay there, limp. He was gliding on a carpet of leaves that brought him down into the hole and, despite feeling like he had spent hours falling into dampness and numbness, in truth it had been no more than a few seconds. He turned his face to the tree and saw it in front of him, then he turned his head to look the other way. He was too weak to believe what was happening, to establish whether he was truly still in the land of the living. As he turned, he saw burning trees, and felt relieved that there were no trees close to each other on that bleak mountaintop. Then he spotted a reddening and blazing in the faraway canopy.

A few specks of mud slid into his eyes, and he could see small, delicate spots falling one after another. He shifted again, and the soil and the trees and the mud moved with him. But where had the mud come from? He shook his head to wake himself and a liquid sloshed in the cavities of his skull. He felt it churn, then the sound moved to the base of his neck and for a moment he imagined that a trunk was growing out of his spine. He was looking at the tree, he was certain he was in front of that oak. Even though he had confirmed this fact time and again, fear was consuming him, beginning with his heart, and it made him doubt what he was seeing. It was a fear he recognised as soon as he remembered Nahla's face—he knew how monsters grow and hide in the eyes of bereaved mothers, how those monsters lie in wait and devour them on cold nights.

Leaves floated down from the branches. He knew what those oak branches were doing! The tree was sending its leaves earthwards, effortlessly ridding itself of them. *Trees enjoy the wisdom of renunciation.* Humayrouna would often say this to Ali, always making him repeat it after her. In the same way, she would say, "I am a tree." So he would obediently repeat after her, "I am a tree." And he would follow her from place to place, clinging to her long, colourful thobe, and she would tell him that she was going to teach him how to be silent, just like the trees were. When he was eight years old, perplexed and furious at her for once again calling herself a tree (a phrase she repeated as often as she breathed), he said to her: "You talk too much to be a tree!" Humayrouna burst out laughing in response and said, "That's because I am not a tree ... *you* are." Nahla used to scold the old woman for talking to the boy like that every time she daubed her son's skinny body with oil inside the maqam. She would rebuke Humayrouna on a regular basis, and Humayrouna would issue swearwords back at her in a vague mumble.

Ali was thinking it now: *I am a tree.* He could smell the scent of the oil his mother used when she rubbed her roughened fingers across his neck. He used to hear her murmuring, imploring God and the saint of the maqam to cure her son of his constant distraction. Then he remembered the strange itch in his stomach every time, and how the pressure of her fingers hurt him and he couldn't even manage to grumble. This sudden memory was no coincidence, he reflected as he rolled his right cheek in the ground, displacing a pile of leaves so he could feel the earth. Then he dug his head down—he wasn't digging really, but it felt as if he could. He had never used a shovel to dig before—he found their arms and their wooden handles skinned his palm—but now he felt that his head was a shovel capable of splitting rock. He had strength enough to force it into the ground, and he scraped the earth near his body and dug up a little soil. These mountains were rocky like the mountains of his village; they were an extension of those mountains. He had never thought of that before. Ali proceeded to dig his teeth into the soil and spit it out, then eat it up and spit it out; he would dig a path towards the tree, moving his head right and left to feel for tree roots, and he would continue turning his head in the soil. Then he heard a sound—it was the rustle of the tree! Or perhaps not a rustle exactly, he thought as he raised his head and saw the head on the other side. That head was moving too, so he pulled his trunk forward, and it was moving ... it was moving, and his elbow began to prop him up, then he flung his trunk forward, and his head crashed into the ground. He knew he was now closer to the tree—not all the way, but he had moved forward and that was enough! He had memorised this tree. It wasn't like the others he had known in his life—the tree of his house or the tree of the maqam. It had been a month since he started living with this third tree—and wasn't it strange that it, too, was an oak? Three oak trees! For a moment he raised his elbow again to progress a little further after biting and spitting out the soil. He was trying to turn his elbow into a stable support, to move his limp body. A sense of ease came over him, difficult to imagine in a young man not yet twenty, who didn't know whether he was alive or on his way towards the other world: a fleeting reassurance. His feelings were exaggerated, impossible to predict. Perhaps it was astonishing that he was comforted, even if only for an instant, but the oak tree was a sign to him; it was taking care of him. And fortunately he was in the mountains around Lattakia—unlike his brother, whose body had been swallowed by the desert to the east of Homs.

Trees were simple, unlike people. This he understood. They were like him, and he believed it when Humayrouna told him he was a tree. He slept standing upright and he understood tree language, though no one else understood the melodies he whistled. He believed that divine care made him move towards the tree, which would protect him from the hyenas ... He was bleeding, he knew he was bleeding, but he wasn't sure where his wound was. His body was completely numb. There was a point of deep pain, though its location was unclear.

That tree in front of him was no coincidence.

He rubbed his cheek in the soil to feel out the roots, thinking perhaps they would tell him what he wanted to know. He told the tree, without words, that he needed to reach it, and heard no reply. The differences between the three trees were gradually becoming clearer in his mind. He thought he must be hallucinating as he moved in and out of consciousness, because the trees were spinning around him. The oak tree behind their house was smaller, because it was young, and in fact Humayrouna used to say that it was still a child, barely sixty years old. Trees grow slowly, so they live a long time, and because they live a long time they grow wise. They have plenty of time to experience living, unlike people who, as soon as they become aware of life, leave it. Humayrouna would tell Ali many such stories in a whisper, and each time she would add, "Ephemeral humans." He was always surprised how someone like her could come out with words like that—"Ephemeral humans!" She would say this in Classical Arabic, then add, in dialect, "Look at that branch, wa'aini ... See how it reaches up to the sky, away from us ephemeral humans." She would gaze and wink feebly, while a swaying thread of light glimmered over her head, breaking through from the little side branch that stuck out from the main shape of the tree, reaching out alone like a small hand coming out of a cervix. And while the light glowed over Humayrouna's wrinkled forehead Ali stared at the peculiar motes that glittered like specks of golden dust among the leaves of the single branch and the blue of the sky. He gave it a brief tap, gazing at the tree, how it had let that branch schism away from its symmetrical roundness and height. And Humayrouna was whispering, "That one's like you, Ali."

Ali remembered where he had been at that moment. He knew where he was sitting, behind Humayrouna's house, which she had built in among the branches of the younger tree, the one ten metres from the tree of the maqam. Ali disapproved of the small tree. He believed it let more light through than it should, and he didn't like the sun's ability to overwhelm it and live among its branches. Perhaps there was a simpler reason: he was never able to fall asleep there. Humayrouna told him it was because he was an idiot; the small tree was his father's age, it wasn't as young as Ali had thought, and anyway, his father was even more of an idiot than he was, because his father didn't understand the meaning of these trees in this sacred place. But Humayrouna remained pleased with Ali, although not with his imbecile father, as she always called him. Ali had acquired the most crucial knowledge of all: the ability to communicate with the air and the soil and the trees. As for water, according to Humayrouna, that was an entirely different matter, and one she didn't want to get into. When she talked about water this way, she would tell him a story about the long-ago days when the Turks controlled the mountains and the coastline, when she left her town to learn the meaning of water and see the vast sea, how she had fled when some men sprayed firewater over the women's faces and beat their men, and since seeing that she no longer favoured the sea. As for why that had happened, she offered no explanation. Ali was listening curiously and wondering how there could be something called firewater, as in his experience water and fire did not mix. Humayrouna was accustomed to rounding off her speeches with the phrase, "Oh, Ali, tree of my heart ... may God never take you into His fire." He recalled that phrase now, and he remembered the firewater, and he saw the fire that was burning the trees behind him. He was certain of one thing: the inner trunk of the oak would withstand the fire. He believed that the old woman's claims were true. Did soldiers burn people?

She used to talk to him without stopping, her fingers fiddling with the blue beads of the misbaha she wore around her neck, and he would flee from her words and his fear of fire and climb the oak. He would surround its limbs with his own and cling to it, and he would close his eyes and swing. She would shout at him to come down, because the maqam tree wasn't like the others, it was here for us to seclude ourselves beneath, not on top of. The time of living in the tops of the trees had passed ... "Get down ... get down, and don't go against the laws of nature. Trees are above, and we children of Adam are below," she would shout, and he paid her no attention. She kept up her harangue as she demanded that he respect the mortal remains of the saints who were flowing out of the earth and into the tree branches on their journey of ascension towards the light, and he would ignore her, dozing off to the sound of her muttering while waiting for a passerby to offer her some food, because then she would share it with him.

When did Ali stop tormenting her by climbing the maqam's tree? Could he no longer remember the moment when he crossed the dividing line between child and man? If asked, he would say it was this moment. The oak tree in the maqam, the oak tree by the house, and this tree that he was now crawling towards—there were differences between them, such as the way the sunlight flaked through them, trivial differences. When it came to the tree at the maqam, no rain could penetrate the branches, even the sunlight could barely break through, and the rustling of its leaves was like a shiver. The melodies of the quivering leaves in the tree by his house were more like a suppressed lament, rising and falling in turn as the wind fooled among the branches. The branches of the maqam's tree were more steady, they didn't utter that frightening whisper at night. He'd never tried sleeping there at night—he had considered it but was always waiting for the right time, to block out the resultant chatter that would inevitably come from the villagers. Deep down he had known that sleeping here would make him appear crazy in their eyes. So far they called him "odd," but no one had yet dared call him crazy. The tree here was different from the other two. The rustle of its leaves was erratic, with no fixed rhythm. Perhaps he hadn't found the right way to hear its particular voice yet. Sometimes it shrieked and at other times it shivered, or swayed its lower branches, letting out a drone like a strangled whisper. There were small twigs growing upwards from the base of the trunk, and in his experience that marked the beginning of the end: this tree was going to die. Perhaps it would take fifty years, but it would in any case die; he could smell it when the soldiers arrived at their post, and he kept circling it like a dog while the other soldiers made fun of him. He knew it didn't possess the smell nor the sound he was used to, that the branches living in the shade below didn't know how to play with light. He would watch the light and he knew what it meant when branches and leaves played with light. In his arzal he would spend hours watching a magical world of colour games. Suns large, small, and all sizes in between, would waver, appear, disappear, leaping high and tumbling down, different at each hour of the light's movement. The sun and moon alternated in the heavens, where light and darkness peeled away, and each of them bobbed and waved among the tree branches like apples. He would reach out his hand when the soft, delicate lines of orange and pink gushed forth, and he would grasp them and they would pick him up in a parachute and scatter circles of light all around him. During the day these circles looked golden and at night they turned silver, and, in between, the motion of colours erupted until he felt his skin colouring too: red, yellow, green, and all their infinite varieties. There was a green whose resplendence altered so minutely that it formed dozens of shades of dark green that eventually ended up black. And a little later, blue formed in a circle around him. Those circles of light soon turned pale blue, then back to green, and at night they turned inky and to a blue that ended up pure violet as he drew his fingers through the quivering leaves, stroking them. In winter, when snow hid the mountains along with the smiles and chapped skin of the farm labourers, he found it difficult to believe everything he'd heard about snow being white. Because the leaves, as they disintegrated under the heavy snowflakes, made him see the world as transparent, a place all colour had disappeared from. He decided that snow had no colour, that it was possible for something to be colourless, like Humayrouna's eyes when they gazed at the sky. He used to call snow "blindness." Ali didn't like people's habit of describing water as colourless; water had shifting, multifaceted colours. He would describe water as a bowl of colours that altered according to its contents.

He found pleasure in paying attention to the sounds of the leaves and making up different names for them, in smelling the wildflowers and running through the forest, playing with light and its transformations, leaping among the rocks. Or waking at dawn on icy days to watch the frosted dew encircling the fruit so that each one seemed to be wrapped up in a crystal ball. He was enchanted by those spheres, those sparkles of light when the sun rose and illuminated the frozen fruit, while the iridescent colour of water shone all around them. At such moments, he would see all the colours in its glow.

Those mountains had been a green paradise half a decade earlier, maybe more. He didn't know what they used to look like, he could only see what was in front of him now. He didn't take much notice when he heard that the mountain was turning to desert; what he saw was no desert, and was more than enough for him. Humayrouna used to say it was natural he should feel like that, because he didn't know the splendour of the mountains in the past. What he could see now was the little that remained; he should have seen this lost paradise a century earlier. He didn't believe her sometimes, he would look over at her and her emaciated body as she drew fingers that had turned into dry twigs over the trunk of the maqam's tree. There, she told him that she always stopped herself from crying in front of trees because she was afraid that the tree would remember. She scolded him once; he had fallen from the topmost branches and hurt his leg. When she saw he was about to cry, she chided him severely, "Don't cry in front of a tree. See how the leaves tremble afterwards? Don't cry in front of a tree. Listen to that sound ... that isn't the sound of leaves, that's the sound of pain."

Now, as he summoned up her words, he was certain he was not going to cry. He was resolved that if he reached the tree, he would tell it what had happened to him. Humayrouna used to say that when trees protect their dear friends, they aren't aware of what they are doing. Trees protect by virtue of their nature—they don't have a say in it. They are like humans, who kill each other because that is their nature. It is undeniable that a tree kills itself when it is alone—the small branches that sprout from below will kill it—but he also remembered that those trees have huge, thick trunks that are stronger than stone. He had spent hours drawing his fingers over the bark. When he came to the frontlines and discovered this tree, he was desperate to touch it. At night, he disobeyed orders, moved outside the sandbag ramparts that stood in his way, and wrapped himself around the tree's bulk. If the gunfire intensified, he simply disappeared around the other side of the trunk. The soldiers teased him, saying that his tree friend had had its chest ripped open by a bullet, but he ignored them. He knew, deep inside, that the tree had not died, that it was protecting him. He was only certain of this before the bomb was dropped in error. Now he was worried, because the trees that warned their companions of danger had burned up, and the oak now remained alone. It wouldn't sense the danger, and therefore perhaps it wouldn't feel him. He looked the other way from the forest. The mountain was burned and there was no end in sight to the ashes. He realised that the strange sound he heard when he regained consciousness was the sound of a tree in pain, not the trembling or rustling of leaves ... He knew the pain of trees, knew it well in cold and heat. Suddenly he could smell something, and it took all his determination and strength to raise his body a few centimetres away from the earth. He saw that being, the Other, that head and torso rising with the same motion, and he threw his body back down again.

The sun was scorching and its blaze concealed many details. It was still in the middle of the sky but he couldn't make out the shape of the being mirroring his movements. Really, he was exaggerating here; it wasn't exactly moving towards him, even though it made the same movements. It was the same distance from the tree as he was, but on the other side, where it seemed very close to the drop. Ali shook his hair, averting his eyes. Then, when he opened his eyes, he understood what was happening and saw a face flying in front of him, hiding the tree from him, a face like clouds, like the mist that accompanied him in the mornings. It was him, he saw himself as though in a close mirror—it was him. He didn't see a sun that burned his cheeks, he saw only his own face. He remembered it belonged to him, it was the same face he had seen in the old well by the maqam, the one he saw in the little mirror hung up in his house, the mirror that used to reflect the sunlight onto the opposite wall in circles of silver. He could even see the colour of his eyes. This was his face. He saw it float before him, then he saw his whole body floating above him and he recognised his green eyes shaded towards blue, and his skinny ribs that looked like dried branches. It was him, with his curly, sandy hair. Now he saw his hair gleaming in the sunshine like the chamomile tisane his mother used to calm their stomach gripes in winter. He was looking at himself, and he suddenly remembered that his head was shaved now. He was looking at himself—shaven-headed Ali was looking at Ali with the thick honey-coloured curls. He wasn't saying anything, just staring into his own eyes; there wasn't a mark on him apart from green and blue sparkles like scattered shards of glass. He looked at himself, and hoped he wouldn't rise all the way to the sky. He had just about reached the point of believing that he was watching his soul ascending to heaven. But his ordinary imagination wouldn't allow him to move, and he could only flutter his eyelashes like the wings of a bird as he saw his spirit flying away, and for an instant he felt there was no need to be afraid of anything. Because he felt nothing, he was a blank, just as he had been before he was born. He knew that he had never thought he needed to be swept away. He didn't need to know the identity of the things around him. He had the kind of relationship with his existence that people called "animal instinct." He had never required all these explanations for his surroundings. He could see birds as they landed on the tip of a branch, swayed back and forth, then flew off before alighting on his palm. For him—as he faced the sunlight, sitting among the tails of the clouds that had the habit of passing over his cheeks—for him, this was a world more delicate than an onion skin, more sternly unyielding than the trunk of the maqam's oak tree. Something he didn't know how to speak about, like the essence of life; he only knew how to look at his surroundings with a sense of intense joy and a colossal capacity for endurance. So he didn't close his eyes. He wanted to see death and glance at his own ribs floating above him. He had grown much thinner in recent months; he and his comrades didn't eat well. That was natural, their commanding officer informed them, because they hadn't secured enough food for the recruits. He considered himself fortunate because he would see everything with his own eyes. Death was like this then; it wasn't so bad, although he had imagined it arriving in some other manner. Then his face evaporated in front of his eyes, and he saw the sun's disc clearly and felt a piercing headache. Instinctively he raised his arm and shielded his eyes with his hand, hiding the light of the burning sun, and then he felt a moment's relief. He had learned that he could move his left hand easily and move his fingers. He brought them up to his pupils, staring wide-eyed through the gaps. A little light slipped through, and he saw the tips of his fingers. They were whole! Bloodied, but whole. He breathed in deeply and turned his face to the tree, then he put his fingers on his cheek, brushing the profusion of blood that was burning his skin, a profusion that was being scorched by the sun. He found that coolness refreshing, the coldness of his fingers as they pressed down on his cheek. Only then did he realise that a searing pain was accompanying the trickle of blood from his left ear, and the chill of his fingers extinguished a mysterious burning that had sprouted somewhere deep, very deep, at the base of his neck.

Chapter 6

He raised his fingers and flexed them, then made a fist on the soil and levered up his torso. It occurred to him that the being was moving, so he turned his face, and saw no trace of it. He lifted his head, and couldn't see it. He tried to remember his comrades' faces—was the Other one of the soldiers, unable to speak? Ali raised his head again and was disappointed when he didn't see the being. So, it wasn't his imagination then? He was certain he had seen the Other wearing military clothes like him. Why would he imagine a uniform? Doubt crept back in as to whether it was himself he had seen. He believed that the sun had stopped him from being able to see properly, but perhaps it was the sun that was making him imagine the being advancing towards him? That being would kill him, for sure.

His breathing was laboured. A few drops of warm sweat slid off his forehead and he felt them go into his ear. Then a liquid convulsed inside his head and colours formed all around him, smothering him like plastic bags, but he wasn't suffocating. He was breathing freely. He wanted to go back to his arzal. That was all he wanted, but what he had to do now was raise himself a little higher and try to see clearly. The sun wouldn't allow him to see very well; he wished it would go down soon. But if it went down, he would be in a worse predicament. Someone was coming to save him, they wouldn't leave him alone on this bare mountain peak to be eaten by hyenas. The forest beasts would scent his blood, and they would eat him whether he was alive or dead. He knew hyenas, he used to see them and had glimpsed the colour of their eyes at night—he had seen them eat cadavers. Animal corpses, not humans, but maybe that distinction was just a matter of time. As for those black birds that hovered in the sky—perhaps they were birds of prey, he couldn't see them properly—that meant there were corpses scattered all around him. He didn't know where the bodies of his friends had flown to after the bomb exploded. He had to get up! He had to move forwards and clear the leaves from beneath him, and sweep all around him with his fingers and his teeth.

He lifted his head higher, breathing in and raising his torso. For the first time, he saw his body completely, half of it submerged in soil and leaves. The other half was unhurt, or so he believed. There was no wound on his chest—maybe he wouldn't die after all? The strike had hit some unknown place, maybe in his ear or the soles of his feet, he wasn't sure. The pain was unclear. How could pain be unclear? He didn't know that he was numb with pain throughout his entire body. He smelled blood, which meant he must be bleeding heavily. His body would fail him because he was skinny and weak; he hadn't eaten in recent months, not even when his stomach had gnawed with hunger. Not once had he eaten enough food since coming to this mountain peak, but he didn't grumble as the others did; he wouldn't have been able to eat anyway, as he had begun suffering from stomach pains. He was familiar with this pain in his stomach; it had started the day he saw a calf running around with only half a head.

That sharp spasm in his stomach then was similar to the pain he felt now. Every site of pain in his body announced itself. Ali reflected that the parallel acknowledgement of both pain and memory was a way of dying slowly.

Yes, he had seen a calf running with half a head.

That day, the men of the village and the sheikhs had gathered to slaughter the calf that Abu Zayn had offered as a sacrifice after the war began. They knew he was corrupt and often whispered as much among themselves, but at the outbreak of the war they were frightened, and they forgot this fact and clustered round him. They were few, most of them were poor, and the graveyard hadn't yet opened its maw to swallow up their sons' bodies. Abu Zayn told them that he would offer a sacrifice dedicated to their sons' souls, for their protection. They knew that his own sons and grandchildren had left the country and only Zayn was left, but they were silent, bereft of power or strength.

The obsessive thoughts that bewildered Ali afterwards were: Did the sheikh's hand slip? Why didn't they pull the rope more tightly when they were tying the calf up? Where did the calf find such strength as it was dying? Such questions kept him awake and smothered his breathing. He saw the men muttering verses from the Qur'an over the knife. He was allowed to be present for that—he was a man by that time. The women, as usual, were banned, and were cooking a number of dishes behind the maqam. He saw the women always at the back, in death and in life, and never considered why it was so. He believed it was part of life, part of nature's cycles, like the sun succeeding the moon. Ali was standing with the men, trying to get closer to the old sheikh while he was performing the slaughter, observing the minutest details of his work. The flash of the knife, the animal's eyes, its neck, the sheikh's fingers, then the blood and the knife's rapid blow. The calf gave a shudder beneath the sheikh's hand. It slipped the ropes that tied its feet, and it kicked the men standing around it in a circle. Ali backed away, and saw that its head was hanging by a strip of skin. A neat little wound in the neck was all it took for the blood to gush out and usually the animal would die quietly, so was the knife the reason? Had it been sharpened too much, and made too wide a cut? Ali would never forget that moment when the calf bolted in his direction and collapsed suddenly on top of him, and he was scorched by the heat of its blood and its warm body.

Ali remembered dreaming about that headless calf strolling over the clouds and screaming at him. The weight of it had nearly killed him. The calf had heaved its last breaths on Ali's chest. He saw its dangling head, and he could smell its blood on his clothes—he would burn them later that night and throw what remained of them down the mountainside. The women had prepared a large black cooking pot that could feed many families. He could smell bulgur wheat, meat, and firewood, and then he remembered the sheikh's fingers as they recorded the names of the destitute families among whom the meat would be distributed. This was all before his brother's funeral. Yes! He recalled Zayn's booming voice as he announced that they were fighting traitors and enemies of the nation. As he pressed his fingers onto his stomach now, he remembered things happening quickly. He remembered the fear of the families around him, the sky that encircled his chest as he heard news of a conspiracy hatched by those who shared the earth and air and sea with them. The villagers called them enemies. He hadn't understood, back then, why they were so afraid. When he asked some other young men in the village why they were scared, they said he was an idiot. This fear caused them to offer up endless sacrifices, and they never stopped offering du'at to God and the President and their soldier sons who were protecting the homeland. Ali was there, observing what was going on as if watching another planet that had fallen out of the sky. It wasn't like that now. He remembered that his stomach cramps began with that incident. The sheikh had fallen to the ground with the knife, which had not been merciful, still in his hand. Then all the families gathered round to take their portions of the meat. Not all of them were there; Ali remembered that a number of men had left the village because, according to Zayn, they were traitors—they hated the President, and whoever hated the President hated the homeland. They had been expelled, and they disappeared into faraway countries, and it was said that others had vanished into prisons. But it didn't matter, because the villagers knew that only three families were affected by their members vanishing, and two of those people had spent their lives in prison anyway; the first had been imprisoned during the era of the father President, the one who died, and the second was still in the prisons of the current President, the son who wanted to live forever. Then rumours started circulating among the villagers that those men had allied with the traitors who wanted to kill them, so it was a good thing they had disappeared, even if one of them was a teacher who had taught all the village children, and even if that man's son was the village doctor, because loyalty to the homeland was more important than any profession, even more important than their children who would die one after another in defence of the nation. It was a strange time back then, when death had only just begun to loom over their houses, and the villagers would still declare, "We are dying out of loyalty to the President and the homeland." Later on, they would stop saying this. By then they would have lost land, and children, and life itself, and whoever was left wasn't so much as able to scrape together enough to cover the cost of their daily bread.

It was around the time of the calf with half a head that Ali heard the first scream, a woman's scream, followed by the first grave in that war that lived in his head. That scream began to go round and round like a rusty key in a lock. A scream like a knife blade. And so everyone learned that the first martyr had entered the village.

He remembered that his stomach had stung him, as it was stinging him now. He couldn't see a calf with half a head, or hear any women wailing, but once again he could smell roasting meat. He raised his torso and lifted his head, and the Other raised his head also. Ali took hold of his sleeve with his teeth and ripped it. He didn't manage to remove his clothes, and only heard his teeth clatter against each other in the attempt. Then a light breeze blew and the rustle of the tree, close by, returned. But the sound didn't appear to have come from that tree, as he had first thought; perhaps it had come from the forest at the bottom of the mountain slope. It was so far away that he thought he was imagining it. He saw the curved leaves from that same oak whirling around him and he delighted in the circles they traced, and he knew it was all a delusion, but to his eyes they looked real. The sun's heat had lessened slightly, and because of that he thought what was happening was real, that he was able to move forward, and that the tree had rewarded him with this light shade of the leaves circling around his head.

If only the tree could walk to him ... but it was fixed in position. It was people who had to walk towards the trees, and he couldn't walk. No one would remember him after this, no assistance would reach him. Suddenly he remembered the comrade who had been next to him at the moment of the explosion. Ali had noticed him flying in the opposite direction—perhaps this comrade was the person he had been seeing on the other side of the tree. But where was his gun? If only he had it—he would feel much better. Then came an image of it flying in the air, landing nowhere near him. Yes, it too had flown away and disappeared. He couldn't see a branch on the ground that he might pick up and use to defend himself. He couldn't even shake off the flies that were gathering round. He spotted a throng of bluebottles, or maybe they were something else? Insects, anyway, swarming over a lump of some kind in front of him. He did his best to dismiss the thought that it was the mangled corpse of his comrade. But not far away, directly on the path he was proceeding slowly along, he saw a hand outstretched: a single, severed hand, and a swarm of flies.

How long had he been there?

He heard a buzzing and noticed flies gathering around the bottom of his feet. Perhaps his feet had been cut off. He would never be able to climb that tree without feet. He wouldn't be able to run through the forest without feet. In fact, he wouldn't be able to stand at all. Then he reached his hand down and touched his middle, trying to pluck his shirt out from beneath the tight belt, but he was too weak so he feebly smacked his abdomen instead; he only wanted to touch his skin to make sure his stomach wasn't torn open. He screamed and the flies, or the bluebottles, moved away. Ali's mind moved to the snakes that might slither past. He wasn't afraid of them. He was afraid of snakes on the open plains, close to the city where he worked with his father, but he had no fear of mountain snakes. There wasn't anything that frightened him in the mountain of their village. This mountain though, despite not being so far from the village, he didn't know at all. He hadn't memorised its animals, he had no relationship with its trees. If he was in his own mountains, he wouldn't be afraid, even if they cut up his body. A tremor struck him, causing him to hear his heartbeat, unaware that memory was a curse. He remembered that the calf had been black with white spots on its forehead, it had been young and beautiful, and it had turned into food in people's stomachs. He hadn't tasted a morsel of the meat his mother had prepared and mashed with wheat. From time to time, as he was sitting on the roof, he would see a slaughtered calf flying in the sky with that same look of entreaty in its wide black eyes as it plunged towards him. It would appear on the opposite mountain peak, cross the space quickly, and land next to him on the roof. Without a word, Ali would flee and race through the village to the foot of the opposite mountain slope, away from their house, where he would stay until night fell.

Ali was so calm that Nahla gave her son the nickname "Al-Hakim"—the sage. She was concerned when she saw him escaping from the roof, running through the paths, and disappearing among the trees, but when she asked him what had happened, he wouldn't answer. She would say he had inherited his muteness from her sister, who had worked as a maid for Abu Zayn, and still Ali would stay silent. He remembered his beautiful aunt who had never married, and whom he never saw standing upright. Whenever she came to mind she was hunched over, scrubbing the stone staircase or cleaning the house, sprawling on the sponge mattress in the bedroom perhaps, or carrying the bags that warped her back. Then one day she disappeared, and they found her body at the bottom of the mountain slope. Ali heard his mother say that she had thrown herself down the mountain; she'd believed she had wings. Ali believed his aunt, because he knew it was true, he had seen her in his dreams, flying with a pair of wings.

If only he could fly to the tree with a pair of wings right now!

Wasn't he like his aunt, after all? Everyone in the village said he took after his mute aunt—everyone called her that, but he knew she wasn't mute. The day before she disappeared his aunt had whispered to her sister about the pair of wings growing out of her back, and Ali thought his aunt must have had her reasons for her belief. His aunt had said that they should all leave this cursed village, and that she couldn't bear being a maid in Abu Zayn's house any longer. Why was he remembering his aunt now? He had thought that there were wings flying him to the tree, but no wings were sprouting from his back, although there was a sort of tickle, like flies crawling, or tiny creatures grazing on his chest hair. The insects were eating him.

Then he would never fly!

Ali stayed on the ground, edging forward slowly, a few centimetres with each movement. If he carried on like this, night would fall before he reached the tree, and the hyenas would eat him alive. *The hyenas won't eat you, you're the one who'll eat them!* a voice said to him, and he knew that he was hallucinating. That wasn't really his mother's voice he'd heard. Ali grasped a fistful of soil, hoisted up his body, and pulled himself forward another few centimetres. He moved his fingers, plunged them into the blood pooled around him, and looked at them. Why was he here? Why didn't he do what the neighbour's son had done and run away? Why didn't he escape? Was it shame? What did shame mean to him? Was it shame or fear, or something else? Was it worth it? Humayrouna had asked him to leave the village before she disappeared. Why did she disappear? Why did everyone keep quiet about her disappearance? Had he himself forgotten her? He had no clue what had happened.

This drone of ideas tormented him. He gazed intently a few metres ahead. He didn't want to believe that those few metres represented all the life he had left.

He sank his teeth into the soil and heard a noise close by. He turned his gaze—it was the being! Four upright black legs appeared, forming the silhouette of a mythical beast through the blazing sunshine. The Other must be animal and not human. Ali relaxed. It wasn't the enemy, it wasn't carrying a gun, and hyenas didn't come out in the sunshine; he wouldn't die until the hyenas came up to him and started tearing at his corpse. The four legs soon disappeared, and illuminated threads settled in their place, and Ali realised the sun was tricking him. He was staring at the being, whose head moved at the same time as his. He had crawled further than he realised because his eyes were looking at branches now—he was getting close. Ali raised his hands and for an instant thought he would run towards the tree, but he crashed back down on the ground. Before he fainted he had retreated a little, and he spotted the hand again. He forgot about the calf with half a head, and in the space of a second he realised that his head had fallen onto a broad, open palm. That second, which was as sharp, swift, and banal as death, was all he needed to be certain that it was the severed hand of his comrade who had been next to him when the bomb fell.

Chapter 7

As soon as he felt the slime of the hand that embraced his head, his lips trembled. Using his shoulders, he scrambled back towards the mountain slope, moving away from the tree.

He slid himself along the ground and got safely away from the hand, and in a moment that repeated over and over like the flowing water in the river at the bottom of the wadi, a moment in which he once again became aware of a pain of some kind, he regained his knowledge of himself, a little more with each repetition, as if he were climbing a ladder, going down new pathways, opening small windows. In this latest renewal of his memories, as he bit his tongue while trying to breathe, he recalled when he bit his tongue that other time. Yes, he remembered now—it had been after the thrashing from the pomegranate cane.

At that time Ali had finished his first six years of school and was about to enter the middle school in the next village. His own was very remote and barely contained a small primary school, so he and the other children had to make the trip there every day. It wasn't an arduous journey, but Ali did not find half an hour on the bus very appealing, and the school walls stifled him. He wasn't allowed to walk there like he wanted. He hated getting in the small white bus and felt suffocated when he was crushed in among the children, but Nahla forced him to do it. Ali, who was now curled up on his side and looking at the tree after escaping the severed hand, could still feel his feet back then, and could run alongside the other children—unlike now. That time wasn't so long ago, maybe seven or eight years, he couldn't remember exactly. He had forgotten how old he was sooner than someone his age usually would.

Ali had made no effort to curb his resentment at being crammed into the bus with children who never stopped screaming and yelling. He submitted to Nahla's wishes and went to school, thinking all the while, why did he have to do what the other kids did, and who decided what it was they had to do? He hated the language of humans, the way they had of speaking and writing and expressing themselves. Quite simply, he didn't like the way they related to their lives—it made no sense to him. Who had decided that he needed to be squeezed in with the others in the place they called a classroom, or in that other confine they called a house? His questions remained locked in his head, however, and Nahla couldn't care less about them. She was determined that her sons would finish their education so they would obtain government jobs, wives, and children. Ali's father was indifferent, or so Ali believed; he believed that his father's lack of interest was valuable, that sometimes it was good to pass lightly over an experience. His father, in this sense, was light, and there were moments when Ali had even loved his father's indifference. He wasn't conscious of using this term—*light*. The lightness that Ali thought of—still did think of—meant, for him, letting time decide, and giving himself up to the elements of nature that he loved. Ali was still captivated by these elements, the wind and the trees, the sky, the clouds, the frozen dewdrops that hung from the branches like chandeliers ... the tiny bees ... the pink worms, and the grasses that sprang up among the rocks ... and then ... all that wasn't important though, because no one would ever understand what he wanted to say; his mother would scold him, and the only mutual language he shared with his father was the pomegranate cane. In truth, Ali was not close at all to the father who left in the early morning and came back in the evening. He never knew what it was that his father did until much later, when he accompanied his father on his trips, and it became clear that they weren't trips at all. The important thing now was that he was recalling that painful blow, so like the pain in his bloody, bitten tongue. Drops of sweat were oozing from his body without pause, and the sheer quantity of them (which he could sense from the saltiness of the gushing sweat that settled in his eyes) made him, when he regained consciousness, even thirstier.

The only thing he could think about was that the pain was unclear. Perhaps, at that distant time, his body hadn't opened up as it had been opened now, but he remembered the blows he received from all directions. It had been his first week of school. His world had changed suddenly, and the new school was teeming with strangers; girls and boys from the neighbouring villages, those who lived in the large village that had become a town. He kept to himself, separate even from the children of his own village. He sat in his chair at the back, as usual, meeker and more serious and silent than a boy of his age should be. He was frightened of *that phrase* and prayed that the teacher wouldn't repeat it, that phrase he heard constantly whenever they were doling out punishments to the children. This mocking phrase stopped him from sleeping, and when he did he suffered from nightmares in which the ground split open and swallowed up the children. He wasn't a disobedient boy—the beatings he received from his father were guaranteed to keep him in line—but that wasn't important, because he wanted to go back to his arzal. If he would only be permitted to leave this world and stay with his trees, he would live happily. It was his dream to see his father turn into a little boy, so they could swap roles. In fact, this transformation was more of an obsession, and he pondered over which miracle would make it happen. One day he interrogated Humayrouna about whether time could be controlled, so that he would grow older and his father would grow younger. Humayrouna told him gravely that it was impossible unless his father died, in which case he would be reborn into another family. Only then would his dream come true, just so long as his father was reincarnated in human form. This she doubted, she declared to Ali, because his father didn't deserve it. Ali didn't like this; he had thought that his father would never die. "Fathers don't die!" he told her woefully, then he was silent about his dream until eventually he forgot it. When he turned twelve, they decided to throw him into this school with all the strangers. He thought the problem stemmed from Nahla, who laid down the law. These strangers were irritated because the kid with the hooked nose and the sandy hair wouldn't say a word to them. For him they were strangers, just as he was to them, and they all crossed vast distances just to squeeze together into cement rooms that the grown-ups called a school.

The first days passed peacefully, even though he found it strange to be among so many boys and girls. For each subject there was a different teacher, which bewildered him. His younger brother, one of the most hardworking students in the village, would explain to him that this was natural because they were growing up and they had to progress, which meant learning more, and more in depth. He reassured Ali that he would follow him to middle school in a year's time, and then Ali wouldn't be alone anymore. Ali's younger, more diligent brother would finish university and raise his family's heads higher. He'd never be forced to end up as Ali has, dragged to a place like this where bombs fell on him by mistake. But back then Ali never paid attention to anything his brother said, and regarded him merely as a little boy. Ali only wanted to stay in the wilderness—even Nahla called him Ibn Al-Barari, "son of the wilderness," or Ibn Al-Dab'a, "son of the hyenas." When Ali announced firmly that he didn't want to go back to school, she said, "Where do you expect to live, Ibn Al-Dabgha, if you don't finish your studies—in the wilderness with the beasts?" He nodded firmly in reply. So she told him that if he did that, he would spend his whole life working as a hired hand on the land of others and he would accompany his father to work on the plains, and he nodded again. When he heard her shouting, he went out into the forest and didn't return until the evening. Instead, he spent the day naked by the river that ran along the bottom of the wadi. He had always loved bathing there, even though the water had dwindled in recent years.

Was there a river here? He had never really had time to discover the place properly. When he and his fellow soldiers went through the forest at the bottom of the wadi to reach the summit, looking for light among the trees, he hadn't smelled any river. They had moved at night, in accordance with their commanding officer's directives. They were on the front line in the Lattakia mountains, where military squadrons that opposed the regime controlled some of the villages. He didn't know anything about these squadrons other than what he had seen in the videos that the villagers swapped among themselves, which showed men wearing long beards and long, unfamiliar clothes, carrying weapons, and threatening slaughter. Although the others had been afraid to be walking at night, Ali had sprung nimbly to carry out their orders, thrilled to be walking through the forest, climbing the mountain, and descending into the wadi. Back then he had both his feet, and he wished he could be sure that he had two feet now, that he could look at them. He could take a look, if only he could straighten his back! But it wouldn't move.

In his second week of school, when he could still feel his feet and he was leaving the world of childhood, Ali was sitting in class, out of the way in the back, lost in thought and oblivious to what the teacher was saying. He felt a slap on his neck and surfaced from his daydream, and he saw the teacher mugging and mouthing, and the children all around him were silent and dumbfounded. He expected them to laugh and make fun of him, but they didn't. The teacher's face was red, then suddenly he heard *that phrase*. The phrase he had been hearing for some time, the one he could distinguish from all the other angry phrases their teacher would spout. By this time Ali had grown a little fluff on his chin, and his moustache had begun to be outlined in gleaming golden strands. He was allowed to travel from one village to another by himself, able to do whatever he wanted. Hair had grown below his stomach, and every part of his body had lengthened, not just his long, hooked nose. His voice had become louder and deeper, and he wanted to kill the monsters that would split the earth and swallow him up, ever since he could remember. He couldn't shout after the pain of the teacher's blow, so only a squeak emerged from him. He couldn't even stutter a response to the teacher's request to read out the text. The teacher snatched up the book and smacked it onto Ali's back, and, for the second time, he said, "Read, or I'll keep hitting you until something comes out of the ground and swallows you up." At that, according to how the other children told it, Ali grabbed his book from the teacher's hand and flung it at the man's face. He leapt over the pupils' chairs, grabbed the teacher's, turned it over, and broke the window with it. The children scattered in terror. Ali threw the chair and the table at the teacher, who struggled to stop him as he, along with all the children, gathered round. Ali was kicking and bucking with his eyes squeezed shut, and if he could have reached the teacher's throat he would have ripped it open with his teeth. But eventually the teacher caught Ali by the neck and the children gathered round to add their own rain of blows. The beating came from every direction, and Ali saw stars falling alongside the teacher's palms, fists, and curses, and if the head teacher hadn't come in and rescued him, they would have likely broken his bones. Ali recalled a question that stayed in his head for years: Why did the others join in the teacher's beating? How did they all gather so quickly? His teacher came from one of the neighbouring villages and was an active member of the ruling party. This was the teacher who would later turn into an activist during the war, one who excelled at assisting the network of militias and Party members. No one knew what he did exactly, and Ali himself would never see him again, but his fame would spread widely. It wasn't just the children who were afraid of him; many people knew his name and repeated it with trepidation. Some said he was the go-between for the powers that be who made the plans and the lower orders who carried them out, others said he was one of the Mukhabarat, but no one knew if the rumours were true. The teacher, who continued to beat Ali until the head teacher intervened, would soon forget the insult Ali directed at him and how it had ruined his standing in front of the students, just as Ali would also forget what it was he had said to his teacher. "Wallahi, there is plenty of cruelty in these mountains but you're the worst of all, you pimp, you bully ... I am the state here!" Even with the passage of years, Ali had failed to learn the shape of this state that he had never seen, although so many spoke in its name. But this didn't mean that he didn't smile, pleased with himself, when from time to time he remembered what had happened at the school, how he had slapped the face of the teacher who wanted to bring the monsters out of the ground to swallow them up.

Straight after that incident Ali left school. Although he was delighted at having fought the monsters who came out of the ground to swallow up children, he stayed in bed for days, but couldn't identify the source of his pain. The black days where he was forced to listen to that phrase were finished, because they never said it at home. He was convinced that schoolteachers were like the forest hyenas and he hated all of them with a ferocity his family found incomprehensible. Once, when feeling brave, he told Nahla that the schoolteachers were spies for the monsters that lived in the ground and swallowed up children. She burst out laughing and paid absolutely no attention to this warning. She thought the matter would pass, just like life all around her passed and disappeared as if it had never been. And so she forgot, and those around her forgot, and even Ali himself forgot a few months after the thrashing. He had regained himself, he thought. He would never be forced to stay in the place they called a school; he would never again have to mix with unfamiliar children who beat him up; and Nahla and his brothers and his father would all forget. The promise of their youngest and most hardworking son, who would make them forget the recalcitrance of their middle child, was a promise that led them, fumbling, towards an aspiration: at last, they dreamed of an educated son who would go to university. Ali would forget that his father tied him to the trunk of the oak, thrashed him with the pomegranate cane, and left him there until night as punishment. Every hour, his father would come and ask Ali if he would apologise to the teacher and go back to his studies, and Ali, tied fast by a rope around his waist, replied only with his customary whistle. He raised his head upwards, ignoring his father and staring into the branches, so his father hit him again and Ali carried on whistling throughout, his eyes fixed on the upper branches and the shapes of the light, absorbed in the games the sunlight played with the leaves. At the end of the evening, Nahla untied the rope and tended to the wounds left by the pomegranate cane, the teacher, and the children, while Ali whistled and whistled without pause.

And now he couldn't whistle. The muscles around his lips were rigid, as if they were tied up with thick ropes. If he was to regain the position he had reached before he scrambled backwards out of fear of the severed hand, unless a miracle occurred, he would have to move faster and lift himself more forcefully than before, because by now the sun had disappeared from the middle of the sky. Using the colours of the light to calculate how many hours had passed, he realised that time was escaping him and so he pushed his chest and his head upwards as hard as he could. He was able to retrain his sight on his surroundings, and before his head fell back he saw those things he called his feet for a few seconds. So then, he still had a pair of feet. They hadn't been cut off. A sudden fear gripped him: What if they weren't attached? What if they were severed beneath that pile of leaves? Then he saw his tall military-issued boots and coughed so hard he couldn't breathe, and he felt something pressing down on his legs. The sensation of weight and the sight of his boots came as a relief; it meant he would be able to walk. But what was the heavy thing that kept his knees from moving? He lifted his neck and something loomed into view, crumpled in a heap. Alarmed now, he once again saw an image of his comrade flying through the air. But after a few seconds he realised that it was only a bag from the remnants of the sandbag ramparts. This meant he wouldn't be able to move forward easily; perhaps it had been the sandbag holding him back. So, he had to get rid of it. He took a deep breath, held it, then moving regularly and persistently he rose as if from the grave, moving his torso from his middle. He flexed his knees and managed to turn his body over. He had done it. He was rid of the sandbag, and his whole body was curled up on his right side. Shaking off the remaining leaves and twigs and the last bits of the sandbag, Ali saw his body was whole, just as he had thought, from the roots of his hair to the tips of his boots.

Chapter 8

Ali didn't know himself. His life came to him intermittently, just as he had lived it. He forgot whether or not he should regard himself as one of those people who lived according to the laws and history of the mountain. It didn't occur to him to consider the shape of his face, his feet, his nose, or to question where these sharp features on his face had come from, or to ask himself who he really was. Or, moreover, why he had to be a part of *all this*. Why should he spend even a single moment on this nonsense that others wallowed in like a limitless luxury, when they knew what they wanted in life and could name it: a hope, or a goal. It was simple, really. Here he was, lying motionless, looking at the tree and the Other. He wasn't focusing on the movement of the sun, or what might happen if it went out and this planet vanished from existence. It appeared that everything was interchangeable, capable of altering suddenly and incomprehensibly. He was interested in trees ... in the wind and the clouds and the mountains, in the rain and the stars, in the moon, the scent on the breeze. He was interested in anything that helped him drown out every sound beyond that call from within, interested most of all in those elements that didn't rely on jabbering, as he called it. As such, he wasn't particularly fond of animals, nor did he pursue birds. The wind had a special place in his soul. He believed he knew the wind even better than the clouds, the rain, and the snow. He used to gulp down the wind and breathe it in when it passed over his cheeks and settled in his open mouth, as if he could eat it up. He would feast on the wind, chewing it and swallowing it down; he could tell the direction it came from with his eyes closed, saw the rain in it before it fell, sensed oncoming snow by how cold it blew.

Yes! The wind was something fundamental to him, as were the trees and the clouds. He had never thought of these elements this way before; he hadn't chosen them, or even consciously recognised them as necessities. He just thought that living among them in this way was life, and felt totally assured that he would never be parted from his trees and his beloved elements. His daily sessions of sitting on the roof of their house in all seasons, away from the family and the neighbours, were a part of his being that no one else knew about. During pitch-black nights, as he lay watching, his ribs moving with the stars, and his soul peeling away like the skin of a ripe pear, he knew he wanted to stay like this forever.

Now he thought that if the wind blew, perhaps he would regain some strength. In an impulse that was exploding like thunder, he wanted to live—yes, that's what he wanted ... to wake up every morning in his village and see Nahla's face, then let the wind stroke his cheek and come to rest in his stomach. This was something deep and vital that he couldn't explain. He didn't even know if he could call it vital, but he could feel it deep down, in his bones.

As soon as he lifted his head with that languid pendulum motion and saw both his boots, his soul surged with wakefulness. Even though he wasn't yet certain whether any life lay ahead of him, at least he could still feel his feet. Thank goodness—this comfort offered him strength! Back into his mind came memories of gentle breezes whose fresh scent wafted beneath his nose. Perhaps the sky would decide to help him and send a gust of rainy wind. But it was summer.

He moved his foot and felt confident that he could sit up. His frustrated hope made him more determined, but as he moved his foot and pushed his head up and leaned on his right elbow, he saw that the back of his boot had a hole, a treacherous blank. The significance of the hole he didn't grasp at first. He couldn't see clearly, despite the dazzling light and his clear line of vision. Then the small gap in his boot became clearer. His right foot. It was his right foot. The boot was open at the heel. Slowly he began to realise that his boot had been mutilated at the heel. He stared, inhaled deeply, and raised himself up so that his torso was half upright. Yes, his right heel was missing. As soon as he moved his foot, soil and leaves got stuck in the bloodied hole, and he felt a pain he had never before experienced. A piece of his body, then, must have flown through the air with the soil and the sand, its pieces scattered.

A part of him really had been buried.

It wasn't a dream.

His eyes swept his surroundings. Perhaps he would find his missing piece. Then it suddenly occurred to him that his heel must have disintegrated permanently. Every new movement brought the discovery of a fresh agony, but the knowledge that he was still alive awakened his determination. This awakening seemed different. He hoped no other part of his body was missing. He would keep on having moments like this, moments of shock and amazement; he would turn his head and see the body of the Other behind the tree, sitting in the same tottering way, leaning on his right elbow, looking at him. Ali would wonder whether the Other had also lost part of himself, maybe his heel. Then a fantasy overwhelmed him that he was looking at nothing but a mirror, that this being was still moving and had the same wound in his left ear. He wished he could see the being clearly, and pull him out of his head. Ali started thinking about the wild animals that would come as soon as night fell. He was ready for them!

What had his flesh looked like as it scattered in the air? It must have been like motes of dust.

Ali bit his lip and tasted salt blended with something as bitter as an acorn. Bitterness with extra salt. He thought briefly that he was like the calf that walked around with half a head; but the thought of the calf brought memories of the wind, and the tree by the maqam, and these inspired him with patience. He knew the wind like no one else did; he used to play with it as it swooped over the rocky precipice. The day after he rejected school and was beaten by his father, Ali leapt up from his bed before daybreak. It was early winter and in the mountains the cold dawn hit people's faces like a razorblade, but the weather didn't stop Ali going out, despite the sores on his feet from the pomegranate cane. He walked across the village and through the forest until the rocky outcrop appeared. Below the rocks loomed a cleft that faced the opposite mountain; the earth was split there, creating a deep slope. The villagers called it the slope to the Valley of Hell.

Ali sat on the edge of the rock and the desire to fly came back to him. He took off his plastic sandals and unfurled his legs in the empty space. He wiggled his toes, blue and scored from the pomegranate cane, and sighed in contentment as the wind played with them. The breeze was cold and cutting, so much so that he relaxed as he lay down and gazed into the chasm below. The sky gambolled with him too, and he was soaked by the rain which had been falling since sunrise. With the tips of his fingers, he clung to the protuberances of the rock, and he looked down to the other side. He wondered whether there was an unfamiliar tree there, one he hadn't met before. Humayrouna told him that there was nothing special there, only a small stream he already knew and sometimes bathed in, and a forest that could be reached on foot from the next village—it was flatter from that side because the mountain slope was less steep. Perhaps he should pack a small bundle of clothes and go down into the wadi and walk until he found a place where he could live without having to come back. An idea returned—he would love to live up high with the wind. He lay back and made his body a right angle attached to the rockface. To someone in the distance he would seem like the base of a right-angled triangle. In fact, he was imagining someone looking at him from above, and this person would see Ali as part of the rockface, his lower half hanging in the wind and his feet swinging in the abyss while his other half clung on, his hands outstretched in a cross, his fingers furrowing the jagged edges of the rock. He wished this cliff would turn into a towering, rocky pillar holding up a bed of stone, with two oak trees next to the bed: the tree of their home, and the tree of the maqam. He relinquished his wish, because the tree trunks would never grow in a lump of rock, but Ali was nevertheless certain they would find some way to extend their roots downwards, pushing through rocky shafts in search of soil. This idea appealed to him, and he smiled. Then he swallowed some raindrops and stuck out his tongue, relishing the taste of the small drops, moving them over his tongue and laughing out loud—something he only did very rarely. Then he forgot the pain in his fingers and his back, the marks on his skin from his father's cane. The cane had been made from a pomegranate tree and was slender and flexible. Earlier that morning, before he slipped out of the house, Ali had anxiously, covetously, pulled it out from under his father's bed where it was stored as though it were a precious treasure. He held the cane in a firm grip and felt how smooth and streamlined it was. He had closed a resolute fist over it and fled to the cliff, waving it in the air all the way, and when he got there he threw it into the wadi and watched it fall while raindrops skipped over his tongue. He needed nothing but his dream of a rocky bed resting on a towering pillar. It should be easy. Once, he had heard a story about a man who lived like that ... and yet ...

The sky had blackened and rain poured down in sheets. Ali straightened up again and swung his feet. Looking into the chasm, he felt no fear. His back was hurting and he couldn't lie down anymore, so he drew up his body and curled his knees beneath his chin, then stood and walked to the edge. He steadied his feet, spread his arms, felt his back tickled by goosebumps (or so he thought) and opened his eyes. He saw the vastness of the sky and the expanse of the forests. He was ready to fly. The wind tempted him to come and play—and he said to himself that playing with the wind meant flying. Ali wanted to join in with the wind's thrilling games, just once without having to rely on the tree branches. He breathed in deeply, swallowing air down until he could feel his bones emerging from his chest, and just at that moment, as the rain hammered down, the wind dropped. Ali woke up from his urgent desire to take flight and moved a couple of paces back from the ledge. He took hold of a sharply jutting ridge of rock that had a plant growing underneath. He didn't look to see what kind of plant it was, but it was thorny and scratched his fingers. Ali curled up in a ball, hugging his knees to his chest, and muttered, "I'm going to live here."

Ali didn't live there. He stayed until nightfall, without moving. When he was tired, he curled up in a ball. His family looked for him all day in vain. Nahla's prayers could be heard all over the village as she screamed into the wadi opposite their house—fearing her son had fallen into the valley and joined his aunt—while his father roamed the forests shouting his name. They stumbled across him the next day. The neighbours said he was unconscious with half of his body hanging in the wind, curled up on himself like a ball of thorns. He had stuck out his tongue and bitten it, and a few drops of blood trickled from the cut. As they brought him back, Nahla swore an oath by every maqam of every saint that she wouldn't make him go back to school. And she made another vow, feasible because it required no sacrifices or money from her. She swore to walk barefoot alongside her son to the maqam of the great saint; perhaps he could cure Ali of his absent-mindedness. She refused to say *his lunacy*, as they did in the village.

Chapter 9

Even in her most desperate moments, Nahla had never before dared to pronounce such a vow. Their living situation had been worsening every week, and the days of offering up animal sacrifices to fulfil her vows were now long gone. But having sworn this oath, she would never retract it. The phrase had slid off her tongue as she removed Ali's soaking wet clothes, waiting for the doctor. "Barefoot ... freezing ... we will walk this path."

Ali was gratified to hear her say this and forgot all about living on top of a rocky pillar. He began to leave his childhood world behind, reassured that his family had yielded to him at last. He imagined what the journey would be like, even though the maqam wasn't very far. Two details appealed to him most of all: they would be walking, and they would be barefoot.

When they reached the city, he saw Nahla bending down and taking off her shoes. As long as he could remember, he'd seen his mother in the same shoes: brown, with square heels that clacked as she walked. She'd bought them from a second-hand shop and always boasted that they were foreign-made. Ali bent down and removed his shoes also. Quickly, Nahla took his shoes and put them in a bag, then took a firm hold of his hand and set off without saying a word.

More than a week had gone by since the incident at the rock face, the entirety of which he had spent confined to his bed. His father warned that the weather was cold and tried to stop Nahla from fulfilling her vow so quickly, but Nahla replied that this was a good omen. Walking barefoot in the summer meant nothing at all—the biting cold was the point of her vow. Many people, Humayrouna among them, tried to convince the scrawny woman to postpone her vow at least until the spring, but Nahla, fearing God's wrath, fretted that her son would be damned forever if she did not fulfil it at once. She added that she would teach her son how to be a man. He had endured the cliff face and the hyenas for an entire night without anything bad happening to him—for her that was a sign. She had to fulfil her vow.

So she gripped his hand with that same resolve, and he remembered how her roughened palm had been firm over his. She pulled him behind her, despite the cold and the abrasions on their feet. She told him that these discomforts were unimportant—the only thing they had to do was follow the highway the government had built between Lattakia and Damascus. Together they crossed farmland and meadows, and for the first time Ali saw citrus groves and the train tracks that ran parallel to the highway, though he didn't see a train in all the time they walked. He was astounded by those iron tracks which no trains ran on. The lemon and orange trees were large, but they could never rival the size of his trees, he kept saying to himself, refreshed at the sight of them. But he noticed they shone with a different gleam under the rain, they had a silver sheen, and their smell opened the veins in his heart. He was enchanted by the vast open space that lay in front of him and the way the grey colour of the sky mingled with the green that covered the land. He didn't know, then, that he was to become a hired labourer on these groves, that he would see them from the inside and discover there were huge orange trees he had never imagined. Instead, he looked jubilantly at the houses and the villages spread out behind them and hoped his mother would reward him with a quick trip to the sea—a trip that never occurred, due to their feet that were cracked and split. Ali was coughing hard all through the walk as he had come down with a bad cold after the vicious chill on the cliff edge. His mother said that this was all part of the vow, and that the more patience he displayed during his pain, the closer he got to God. From time to time she added that when Ali grew up, he would understand what it meant to please God and the saints.

When Ali reached the maqam, he looked at it in some astonishment. It was nothing like the picture he had traced in his mind of wind and trees. It was nothing like the maqams in the mountain uplands. It looked a bit like a guesthouse.

Together, Ali and his mother stepped through the maqam entrance, each using their right foot to cross the threshold. Then they kissed the wall on the right-hand side, kissed above the door, kissed the left wall, and finally stepped forward humbly. The bliss Ali had expected to feel on arrival was missing. Yet here he was, lying down next to the tomb covered with a green cloth, fixing his eyes on an open, circular window through which tree branches could be seen. Nahla rubbed his face and his feet with oil while sympathetic people offered them food and drink. Mother and son were exhausted, drenched with rain, struggling to breathe, and the laden sky decided it that they would stay overnight. Nahla was doubly resolved that she would not walk back that day when she saw her son's feet.

These were the feet Ali was thinking about now, as his feet and his missing heel had brought back memories of the rock face and the maqam; the same toes he couldn't see while lying down, although above the tip of his soldier's boot he did see phantoms of blood and shredded flesh flying in all directions. But there, in the maqam, he could still touch the cracks in his heels, the wounds on the soles on his feet—back then, he was whole. When his mother wrapped a green robe around his chest and rubbed his face with oil, which had been blessed by having verses from the Qur'an recited over it, she said the phrase she would repeat time and time again: "My son is in your hands, Sheikh Bou Ali ... may it please you to bless us ... my children ... my flesh and blood ... with every step I took in raising them, I fulfilled my vows ... I raised them with my own flesh and blood ..." Then she held out the green blanket and wrapped it again around Ali's body, and its warmth stole into him. The voices of the maqam's visitors were muffled and imploring, the roof of the dome was not too high, and its walls were clean and white and lined with pictures, and copies of the Qur'an were distributed. Contrary to many maqams, whose saints had only a ceremonial tomb inside, this saint—*quddus sirrahu*, as the sheikh always said—was buried here. Ali clung to the tomb as a shiver went through him. He wasn't afraid to sleep next to a grave rebuilt from marble. He thought about their village's maqam, built of cement, and which he liked to call Maqam Al-Rih—the maqam of the wind, or where the wind calls home. It had been built at the highest point of the mountain. The right wall was jammed up against the trunk of the oak tree that the villagers said was more than five hundred years old. The tree branches embraced the maqam like the palm of an outstretched hand, covering the building's dome. Others spread out and upwards—these were the branches he climbed sometimes, and from the very top he would observe the mountain peaks. He had often heard his mother say that they were living just below God's dwelling place; this made him feel special, as though he possessed a secret that was his alone. His maqam, Maqam Al-Rih, was small, clean, and painted with lime. Its modest tomb was covered with a single piece of green cloth, and inside it visitors could find earthenware jars of oil and incense. In recent years, Abu Zayn had presented the maqam with a painting of the saints that included the President the Father among their number. It was a large portrait about a metre square, and it was hung in the centre of the wall. Each man's face was separated from the next by a halo of white. Ali was born seeing this picture and it had always confused him. When he was five they told him that these men were the virtuous saints. Whenever he looked at the faces, he would try to trace some resemblance between each of them. He didn't understand why the President the Father was different; he wasn't wearing a turban or an iqal like the others in the picture did. Why was he among them? Why was he pictured in this way, raising his hands to his ears like he was praying? Ali loved one of those saints in particular, and had grown up gazing at him. He preferred him to all the rest. This saint's face was illuminated by colours that opened up a window in his heart, even though these colours only shaded between white and black. There were thirty-nine sheikhs and walis in the picture. The President was in the penultimate row, and Ali's favourite was in the first. Whenever Ali entered the maqam, he would look at him and address him. He believed this saint was the most worthy, and was fascinated by him, quite apart from the colours of the painting, which were mostly white. He was entranced by the saint's wrinkles, his thick white beard, his emaciated appearance, the hollowed-out cheeks that made his face sad and ascetic. He was six when this secret love story was contracted between himself and this face. He asked his mother once if the saints had Presidents too, or if their President was like the saints. Were they all Presidents? His mother didn't answer. She shot him a sharp look, then turned her face away, saying, "I see you've grown a tongue and learned how to talk. Now get out of here."

After that, he stopped mentioning the matter. He was too young for that. He stopped staring at the picture and he no longer cared that there was a picture of the President among the saints. He memorised the picture of his saint and would look at it when he was by himself. The picture was inside him while he leapt nimbly from rock to rock. They used to call him the *mountain goat*, which made him laugh. He would spring even more lightly among the rocks in defiance of their mockery, and he never felt the insult of being called a goat—on the contrary, he quite enjoyed it. Ali felt that every insult he'd received in his life had come in that marble maqam, while he was covered with the blessed green cloak, dozing off from his exhaustion and wounds. That insult, in which his mother saw a type of salvation, a sign of God's satisfaction with him and with her vow, had begun as Nahla was using her thobe to wipe down Ali's feet soaked with blood and oil. He remembered that she had rubbed his heel. He could feel her touch now, and marvelled how, although years had passed and he had forgotten those moments, they were coming back to him, so strongly that he could feel her touch even on his severed heel. She was rubbing his feet with oil, and he was woken from his sleep by stabs of pain. The balls of his feet still bore the marks of the pomegranate stick, and the long barefoot walk in the rain had made his wounds split open again. Then Nahla took hold of his face and she rubbed it with oil, repeating, "My son is in your hands, Sheikh Bou Ali ... may it please you to bless us ... my son ... my flesh and blood ..." She kissed Ali's toes and licked the blood off them and wept. He would remember that she, like him, had often been beaten with the same pomegranate cane, and from time to time she would escape sobbing to the corner of the second room. Nahla was not good at reading and writing, and his father barely knew the alphabet. He used to scream at his wife to educate his sons, and he beat her when he discovered that she had not, forgetting in his rage that she couldn't read or write. Then he would beat her for reasons that were not kept hidden from Ali, such as the times she stopped her husband from lying on top of her because the children were sleeping close by, and she knew her belly would swell up again and out would come another pile of flesh to torment her heart and break it in two, just like Ali and his siblings. She always used to say that her love for her children would kill her, so Ali didn't stop her from kissing his toes.

In the scene that followed, a scene no one else would consider an insult, Ali was insulted. It was a feeling that remained unacknowledged, and he didn't describe it to himself as such; to himself he described it as feeling like someone was stepping on his neck. He was curled up around himself, nestled against the tomb, and he wished his mother would stop crying and licking his wounds. The insult settled deep inside his heart when he heard a man say, "Get up and get out of here, you madwoman. Someone take her outside, and may God grant us sanity and religion, O Lord." It was the same man with a subha in his hand that Ali had spotted out of the corner of his eye a little earlier. He was a sheikh, but not the sheikh of the maqam; he was one of the new sheikhs that had sprung up in recent decades. The sheikh of the maqam, who appeared later on, seemed like a kind man, or so his mother recalled afterwards.

The incident unfolded as Nahla was holding the Qur'an in her hand and kissing her son's feet, asking him to recite from it for her. The man with the long misbaha was looking at them both, then he tore the Qur'an out of Nahla's hands, shouting, "This woman is not pure. Get her out of here, go on, turn her out!" There wasn't anyone who would carry out his words; it was a sacred place, and the weak and the poor had the right to anoint themselves there, but a woman coming with blood visible on her dress would not be permitted. The blood smeared on her thobe was Ali's, but the sheikh thought it was from her period. Ali didn't understand what was happening, but he felt the man's revulsion, and his mother's as well; Ali curled into himself and closed his eyes. He was exhausted, and a slight fever was beginning to course through his frail body. The sheikh's strident voice resumed, ordering Nahla to leave the maqam. Ali, hearing the rain pouring down outside and the sheikh's furious hectoring, curled up even tighter; to the people gathered in the maqam, he looked like a boy of twelve, brought there to be healed of some kind of mental infirmity by his mother, who seemed a vagrant. On their arrival, she had said to the circle of people around the tomb that her son was not like other children, he was always distracted and believed he was a tree, and so people called him *idiot*. She knew that her son was not an idiot—all he needed was a blessing from the saints—and her audience helped her. One woman wept alongside her and muttered some verses from the Qur'an, placing stones from the maqam onto her swollen belly and passing them gently over Ali's head. Another woman took Nahla in her arms and patted her shoulders. They let Nahla do whatever she liked, because God embraces all his children, however wretched. Then, the moment that the maqam was emptied of its crowds, the man with the subha shouted at Nahla. Ali was on the verge of falling asleep, but his mother reached out, kissed the sheikh's hand, and handed him the Qur'an. As she turned her back on the tomb, she burst into tears. Ali had woken up by this point, and he turned to the sheikh with a look that his mother was very familiar with. Ali sprang up and dealt the sheikh a single blow. The sheikh fell to the ground and took a few seconds to emerge from his shock. In those few seconds Ali pounced onto his chest and wouldn't stop punching until some men pulled him away and dragged him outside, to the shock of those present. Ali kept looking at his toes, ignoring the onlookers.

He had a history with those toes.

The maqam had to be entered with bare feet, so Ali used to spend hours with his back bent over the wall of the tomb, stretching out his feet, observing his toes, playing with them, relishing the cold. He used to plant his toes in the earth of the maqam, and he would be struck with a rare sense of weightlessness and illumination. These feelings carried him naked on a gentle breeze, as if he were one of his clouds, and those moments, when he dissolved just like the clouds did, used to grant him a feeling of the freshness and sweetness of being alive. Humayrouna used to tell him that every maqam sleeps in a tree trunk, and so he felt as though he were flying whenever he entered one. The maqams were blessed, guarded by the holy trees that remained steadfast for hundreds for years. But Ali wasn't really interested in what Humayrouna said. He was like all the others, despite being devoted to her. He would drift off as she gabbled on, apart from when she told the story of the toes, which he used to believe turned into roots or branches upon entering the maqam. He felt the same sensation of weightlessness and freshness when he climbed trees and leapt on rock bluffs, until he thought that one day his toes would stick to the branches and become one with them. A few times he experimented by standing on a branch and raising his hands like wings, steadying his body with his toes, like a hawk did with its talons. He managed to show the villagers who were visiting the maqam how to walk over trees like a bird without falling, and how to steady their legs on the branches or turn upside down and swing like a bat. He felt this same lightness when they pulled him off the body of the sheikh, and his mother was looking at him in horror, expecting to be thrown out into the cold night. His toes were attached to the ground of the maqam in that rare way he had memorised and he wasn't angry at all, he was merely panting and looking at his mother, reaching out his hand, and he stroked her hair very tenderly. His face was calm. The sheikh responsible for the maqam came outside, took the boy's hand and raised his head. Ali got up with his mother, but he couldn't stand, so the sheikh picked him up and told Nahla to follow them; she and her son would spend the night in his house. This sheikh looked at the toes of the boy, who breathed as if he were choking, looked at the confident calm in his eyes, and recited some Qur'anic verses over him. The sheikh directed no rebukes at anyone; he entered with grace and left with dignity. Ali observed his face apprehensively. It resembled the face of his beloved saint in the painting in the Maqam Al-Rih, the maqam of his village. This sheikh had the same air: wan, emaciated, bearded, and with a deep serenity in his eyes. Ali became overwhelmed and forgot the pain in his feet. He surrendered his head, resting it on the sheikh's shoulder, ignoring his shame about his toes.

Ali had always been embarrassed about his toes and did his best to hide them. They forked off like tree branches of different sizes, one short, one long. The toes of his right foot weren't the same length as the toes on his left, and his big toes were the smallest of all. Now, looking towards his boot to see if his toes had also scattered in the blast, he saw his missing heel and remembered the toes that the sheikh had stared at when he carried him. He moved his right foot, straightened his torso, spread out his legs, then slowly reached out a hand. He could feel his ribs were broken, so he moved even more slowly, trying to pluck the last clot of sand, leaves, and twigs away from his knees, when his boot appeared to him, just as it had always been. His toes were still inside, although the layer of mud and dust covering it had turned it from black to white. Ali dragged his body forward using his elbow, and saw that his blood had turned the ground beneath his heel into a mire. Only then did he believe that maybe he had been hit somewhere else, somewhere he couldn't feel yet, and he would only realise when he saw it.

Chapter 10

Dreams, which could be described as shards of light among the motion of leaves, were for Ali that simple thing that others called *home*—the place where they shut their eyes in comfort and peace. People spent their whole lives arguing over what to name that place as they careened towards extinction, and Ali did not challenge them. He wanted no part in the constant debates and quarrels over what people meant, what they understood, what they were talking about. He listened in silence, the few times he was fated to find himself among them.

Ali's home was his arzal. Whenever he referred to it, that was what he called it: *home*. He had constructed it himself out of his beloved elements, which he called his friends. He gathered tree branches for building materials, and the floor was formed from the oak tree itself, whose branches reached out in a circle rather than upwards like the oak tree at the maqam. They were spread like a cupped palm, staying close to the earth. If Ali wanted to describe a tree he would hold up his palm and move it with his fingers to describe its shape. The villagers often said that the men who rebelled against the Turks and the French had passed the tree where Ali had made his arzal. Inside the tree, where the trunk began to fork, three revolutionaries had slept as they escaped French troops. A century ago a newborn baby had been found by that trunk; here also, more than half a century ago, great men had held meetings, coming from Damascus, Hama, and Aleppo to discuss the future of the country—all stories and rumours that Ali paid no attention to. What mattered most to Ali, when he began building his arzal, was that he worked with the zeal of a hundred men, listening to the loud thudding of his heart. He spent days gathering small twigs and larger branches. After the incident at the maqam, his family had given up on him and left him alone to do whatever he wanted, although his father had told him he had to get ready to join him working in the plains. Ali didn't think that would be so bad, and at least it wasn't what the other children were doing. He began to plot long trips through the forests, then made a list of the work he had to do each day. First he had to make a rope ladder that wouldn't hurt the tree trunk. Next, to construct a wall out of tree branches. The last wall would be left open, looking out over the mountain peaks all the way to the end of the sea.

The villagers saw him going back and forth on the paths and slopes, disappearing into the forest and returning loaded with branches. He appeared to have grown twenty years older overnight. Ali didn't strip the branches down to form an even, orderly wall; instead, he left the twigs and leaves on and weaved them in and through each other, the delicate with the hefty, the middle lengths with the long, all entwined together like a tapestry. His first job—gathering the branches—took an entire day and he returned with a face full of scratches. He spent two days under the oak tree braiding the branches together, tying them fast using hemp ropes he found carelessly tossed to one side in their house. These ropes were from the years when they used to grow balady tobacco. To cure the leaves, they would thrust them onto sharp needles then hang them up inside their house. Ali needed to whet the needles with stones sharp as rusted knives, then he threaded the ropes through their long cylindrical holes. He bound the tree branches together in the same way he used to see his mother stitching together their plastic mats.

After Ali finished making the first wall, he fixed it firmly in place with the ropes he brought from the maqam, tying the tips of the wall to the tree branches. He scrubbed the floor of the arzal so it was smooth and not at all rough like the rest of the trunk. He wouldn't need anything more than a light cover on snowy nights; his quilt would be enough. But he was already sharing it with his younger brother. This was an obstacle, as buying anything new in their house required lengthy planning. He put off thinking about this problem and lay contentedly in the tree's lap, and the following morning he woke to find his fingers punctured all over from the previous day's labour. Meanwhile Nahla, who had been observing her son with pity as he was hard at work, noticed the faint fluff that was growing above his lip. She gathered up some of the blessed green fabric that she'd brought back from the maqam, and added to it the old clothes that the maqam offered to the needy. Ali watched from the corner of his eye. She used various colours and types of fabric, linen and wool and cotton, even scraps of denim; she cut out squares, triangles, circles, flowers, and leaf shapes in different sizes, then she sewed them all together using white quilting thread. She waited for him to finish his task and leave for the forest so she could climb the tree and measure the required space, then she went back to sewing the pieces in her own unique way, where she stood up and sat back down again with every stitch. To others she looked ridiculous, as if she were bobbing up and down in a peculiar dance; her husband mocked her for it, but she ignored him. They were all surprised on the fourth day because as soon as Ali climbed down from his arzal and was out of sight, she climbed up carrying his pillow and his thick quilt. It was a gem, everyone said. Her youngest son said she had made a piece of art—and she always said he was the smartest of them all. His comment made her believe in herself. He had climbed the arzal and was taken aback at the finesse and beauty of the blanket. Even though her youngest son was her great pride in life, it didn't stop her from yelling at him to get down before Ali got back. Meanwhile the youngest son was complaining that the tree didn't belong just to Ali, and Nahla replied that his school was enough for him—everyone had their own world—and the tree was Ali's. Ali didn't say a word when he saw the quilt. Ever since he'd first seen Nahla sitting and working without pause, thrusting her needle into pieces of fabric, moving her hands acrobatically among her white threads, beside a pile of shabby clothes that she had washed and hung up to dry on the tree branches, Ali had known she was making something for him. The following evening he asked her to climb up and see the sky from his arzal. She was the only one he allowed to do so. When she climbed up and sat next to him, she didn't cry as she usually did. She smiled briefly, and kept watching the sunset without saying a word. When she left him, she decided the time had come to speak to the sheikh about preparing Ali for learning his religion, and serving the maqam in the coming years. Ali had asked her to do this after their recent visit to the faraway maqam. He had decided to follow the path of the man in the portrait, his beloved saint with the faintly concerned air.

Ali was lying down in his arzal. He liked to close his eyes when they were submerged in light. He didn't appear to experience those lyrical feelings that might be attributed to a boy who enjoyed a close relationship with the natural elements. He had no idea about any of that. His skin was too rough for it, his soul was like the rocks of his mountain, but he could easily close his eyes as he teased the scattered leaps of light when they wriggled through the branches. He would move his head, following them like a dog catching a bone, and he never stopped laughing. Nahla would hear him and weep for her peculiar son—what sane being played with light? He never understood why she was so troubled by his games with the light or with the movement of the wind through the branches. She forced him to carry a ktiba above his heart, and she herself hung it around his neck on a hemp string. This amulet consisted of a small rolled-up piece of paper on which incomprehensible writing had been traced in blue ink, wrapped in a pouch of green cloth from the maqam, which had been blessed. Ali opened his eyes as wide as he could, imagining the trees of these mountains running and scaling the peaks like a herd of goats. He would see their roots that had been plucked from the earth dragging giant rocks behind them, roots that turned into toes like his and walked and ran, and he was on top of his tree, which swept him along with its arborescent herd. He didn't tell anyone his secret, that he had led an army of trees as they galloped up to the sky. He could see that multitude as if he were sitting on one of his clouds, could see them running ... running with their huge, liberated trunks and their colours glowing silvery green and turquoise. That huge flock of trees never looked back. It climbed and climbed, but it didn't reach the mountaintops, never came close to the sky, no matter how hard it tried.

Now, he had moved close to the tree, and the sun was brushing against the opposite mountain peak on its descent to the sea, allowing him to see the trunk clearly. He remembered smiling on top of the arzal at that army of trees, and through his weakening sight, he remembered that there was a place to lie down in, a little like his arzal. This tree rose upwards, and it didn't seem exactly like his oak; it seemed younger. He was always able to guess the age, history, and type of trees. As for where this knowledge came from, the villagers used to say that Humayrouna had shared her secrets with him. Leaving their gossip aside, he had touched his hand to everything he saw in the woodland, touched it and held onto it and grown up with it. He held knowledge about the movement of plants and trees that was known only by the wild animals.

Now, he was trying to crawl, using his elbows, staring at the earth below him, longing for his arzal. He remembered how Nahla climbed up to it the night they buried his older brother, and how he stayed at the base of the trunk guarding her as she sat without resting her back against anything, hugging her knees to her chest, curled up like a hedgehog. He dozed off briefly, then woke up to watch her, and spotted her still in the same position. He was at the base of the tree, standing up without break, not daring to move, staring dry-eyed until he drifted off for a second. In the morning, she woke him with a gentle touch then went into the house. He climbed up to his arzal and stayed there, watching the sky. His favourite quilt was in a heap, just as he had left it the night before. He felt cold and thought of Nahla who had stayed up there all night without a cover. He thought about her now, as time lengthened while he was trying to crawl on his elbows, and the tangled tree branches and segmented leaves waved and formed a roof over him. Perhaps he should try to strip off his soldier's boot and bind his wound that was so much more than a wound in his flesh—but he wasn't sure, and couldn't know. Perhaps it was fortunate that he couldn't sit up and take off his boots. He buried his face in the earth, groaned, swallowed the soil, then spat. Into his mind sprang the forest hyenas whose voices he used to hear up in the arzal. He would watch them as he set alight piles of firewood to drive them away. Just when he thought he would die, he saw Nahla climbing up to his arzal and staying there all night, alone with the cold, just as she had done when they buried her oldest son. Some unknown force assailed him the moment he recalled the image of her bowed back. She was so thin that her back seemed like a bow arced into a semicircle, and he recalled that she was wearing a black woollen tunic. She had wound a white scarf around her face and head, and he knew that her cheeks were cracked, and she stammered when she spoke because she was ashamed of her teeth, which had been broken from the time she fell down the nearby slope—only a tree branch had saved her from falling into the depths of the wadi. He remembered her teeth now, the way they chattered when she was angry, and his eyelids began to droop. He saw the interlaced branches of his arzal close by, circling overhead as he had never seen them before. They were beautiful, and he was filled with contentment at the quality of his work. Even their neighbour said it was skilfully done, and that Ali was an artist. Ali remembered laughing furtively to himself at that comment, but he didn't show that he'd heard what the man had said. He saw himself as a boy, spinning around with the branches now, and he also saw the quilt flying and dancing with the wind. He was so proud of his mother who had fingers of gold, as the neighbours used to say. He reached out to take hold of the blanket and grasped emptiness, and he toppled over onto his stomach so that his back was open to the sky. He screamed feebly. A new pain appeared in his left ear and he knew he was injured somewhere else as well, but the image of the arzal and the tree had grown so close and clear there was no doubting them. He launched himself forward, and with that push a phantom of the arzal appeared, exactly as he had known it for years, decorated with plants and the tin pots that Nahla had filled with basil and thyme. There were the dangling hemp ropes he had hung between the branches, woven together like a mat that held the oddly shaped rocks he collected from the forest. Dangling and swinging they let out a sound like music as they clinked together in the wind. And before he closed his eyes, he once again spotted Nahla with her bowed, trembling back. He remembered that the incessant sinking and lifting movements of her spine were accompanied by stifled gasps. With each movement of her sobs, her back would gently touch the wall of the arzal, and every time the wall touched her back, the dried leaves would rustle, just as they were doing now, all around him, whenever he tried to move.

Chapter 11

Nahla's bowed back was the last thing he remembered before he lost consciousness. When he awoke, the orange sky was fading to nothing, and the tree looked to him like a black silhouette. He needed a few more pushes in order to touch the trunk, and he had to climb it before night fell and brought with it the familiar blackness. The moonlight, when it came, wouldn't fail him, and he would use it to see the shadows of things. The moon would be full on this day of the month, and although it hadn't come out yet, it must be somewhere.

He raised his head, looking for the Other. His spirit? His enemy? He was so close to it now that its outline had become clear. He could see a man's head, and he could smell the fear coming off it. It was frightened of Ali!

How had Ali acquired this power? How had he been able to gasp now and come back to life?

He could see Nahla!

She was here, standing beneath the tree, bending over and reaching down to the quilt she had made.

On the night of her son's burial Nahla stayed sitting, sobbing without tears, breathing slowly. She stopped up her rage and bound her eyes with a cloth and refused to weep. Ali knew what she did not know about herself. Afterwards she opened up to him, just as Humayrouna had. Nahla had married at twenty. Once, she had been an average-looking girl, the seventh of ten siblings who went down from the mountains to work on the plains after her father stopped growing tobacco. Her siblings—along with half the village—left and wandered off in all directions, ending up distributed across a few different cities. Most of them settled in the outskirts of Damascus or emigrated to find work in Lebanon, while those who remained worked as hired labourers in the villages by the sea. New kinds of tobacco were planted on the plains, as opposed to the balady tobacco that was cultivated up in the mountain.

Nahla used to go down to the plains to work in the new tobacco fields, sown with the Virginia and Burley varieties. They left at dawn and came home at sundown. Scrawny, wiry Nahla didn't believe she would ever know love. She thought of nothing but the happiness that had flooded her when she was approached by a man fifteen years her senior, a hired hand on the plains, as was she, who said he wanted to marry her. She thought it would be the end of her misery, and only learned about his abject poverty after she married him. She bore her husband six children, the first of whom died a few months after being born. It was God who heaped gifts on her in the shape of her children—and she didn't dare to complain about God's blessings. Her husband, who worked like a bull, as she always said, would remind her with a sneer that if he hadn't married her, she would have remained a hired hand. She used to mock him by pursing her lips, twisting her neck, and looking away. Nothing in her life changed after her marriage, except her belly swelled up on a regular basis and she had to care for the hunks of meat that kept turning up in her house. She used to declare: "God, the Giver of Gifts." The hunks of meat, as she called her flesh and blood, were her secret delight, but she believed that if she expressed joy at seeing her little ones growing, it would summon bad luck, the evil eye. Things were fine, she thought. Her oldest son had obtained his high school baccalaureate with a mark she was proud of, and since they didn't have the money to send him to university, he had enlisted in the army. This made Nahla proud; her son would live in the capital, he would see things in the world that she never had. Her middle son, Ali, may have his eccentricities, but she believed he would be a pious man of religion. This pleased her so much that she singled him out for sacred care. As for her hard-working youngest son, he was the joy of her life. He would complete his university education, and his brother in the army was guaranteed to help them bear the expenses of the days to come. She had married off one daughter before she was seventeen, and the other was still studying and seemed to be following in the footsteps of her diligent brother. Nahla wanted her daughter to become a doctor like some girls from the village had done—she wouldn't live the wretched life of her mother. Nahla would send her to her brother in the capital in order to study. She had settled it all. Her children's lives were already arranged in her mind and she was confident that, despite their poverty, they were capable of being good, virtuous children. And she herself was still strong, she would go down to the plains with her husband and continue working. It was an orderly world in her head; harsh and dry, but it was enough. Nothing else mattered to her.

She used to work without stopping; they gave her the nickname Kadishat Shughl—workhorse—and her reputation preceded her. And just as they said, she didn't straighten up once from dawn till dusk. The instant she arrived she took hold of the mattock and started work, breaking up the earth. When she worked on the tobacco plains, she would be seen to work in silence until lunch. The other workers would stop to eat, but Nahla would merely chew a crust of bread with oil and salt and then carry on impaling the tobacco leaves, indifferent to the hostile glares of the other workers who felt pressured to do the same when they saw her working without pause. Nahla felt driven to toil and toil. She cherished the hope of putting away a little extra money in case the work dried up, but this extra money never materialised: she and her husband could barely manage to plug the rumbling stomachs of the hunks of meat. Ali recalled her at dawn, preparing the bread rolled up with oil and zaatar before they went to school, sweeping around the house with a straw broom she had made herself. For her it was a basic necessity that a house was clean and smelled nice, and Ali remembered that their ancient clothes were always anointed with the smell of laurel and wild thyme.

When Nahla's children were young, it was her husband's habit to beat her in front of them. After they grew up, he used to beat her in secret. Once, Ali had bitten his father while he was hitting his mother—bitten him and punched him. Even though this earned Ali his own portion of stings from the pomegranate cane as well a stretch left tied to the tree trunk, his father began to exercise prudence and didn't dare beat Nahla in front of him again.

After the funeral and the night in the arzal, Nahla stopped working in the plains, and Ali's father stopped yelling, and his widowed sister stopped weeping and wailing. Ali remembered how silence enveloped the house and Nahla did what he could never have imagined: she cultivated the rocky slope at the bottom of their house and turned it into little terraced steps—even though this was men's work. She hammered the rocks and crumbled the stones with a heavy axe and she built the terraces. She would roam the surroundings of the village gathering empty tin cans, then she'd fill them with soil for her flowers. She would pull up the wild plants in the forest by their roots and transfer them to her astonishing flowerpots until the house was surrounded with them. Over the months, she transformed their house into something like a farm, filled with all kinds of foliage. Ali recalled that she moved the soil from the neighbours' lands and emptied it into the terrace. He was overjoyed as he watched her moving soil, creating crucibles of parsley, mint, radish, onion, and pepper. She planted apple seeds and when they became seedlings, she transplanted them along the paths leading to their house.

Nahla never once went back to the graveyard where her son lay buried, and refused to join the women of the village when they went to visit their sons' graves. They continued to urge her to follow their example until the day she chased them away and threw the branches of myrtle she was carrying at them. Ali didn't remember ever hearing the sound of her voice after his brother died. When his father came back alone from the plains and told her that the patrol had got hold of Ali and taken him away to the army, she screamed a single sentence at him, "May God smite you, you should have killed them all before you let them take him." Then she would resume her silence, having prevented her husband from hitting her. He never again dared to raise a hand against her. In front of others he would feign authority over her, but after his oldest son died he took to weeping at her feet and pleading with her to speak to him while she stood in silence like a stone statue and averted her eyes.

He remembered her clearly ... Skinny, indefatigable Nahla. The whiteness waved at him; white had been his mother's favourite colour in his last days in the village. He used to hover around her like her shadow, helping her as she painted the house with white lime. She scrubbed the walls vigorously and repainted them both inside and out, then she painted the plant pots and cans and the small white stones that she lay in two lines to create a pathway to their door. She would point and gesture to him with her fingers, muttering without directing any speech at him, that this white would be close to the souls of the saints and it would lead her son's soul to her. Whenever Ali tried to speak with her, she ignored him and wouldn't look him in the eye. He thought of her white fingers and his own fingers. They would work companionably side by side while his siblings looked on in silence. Silence became part of their life. Ali could remember those moments, his mother washing the walls inside the house, then repainting them again with lime, and so on ... She did this over and over, and no one dared stop her. Ali recalled that she spent a lot of time underneath his tree, staring at the sky through the branches. And she picked up a new habit: cleaning his arzal, collecting more strange stones, tying them with hemp ropes to the small twigs in the wall of the arzal. Then she would disappear to the mountain and come back with her various plants and stew them for her children. By the time they seized him, on the day when Nahla called God's wrath down on her husband, she had planted enough vegetables that she no longer needed to buy any. Ali had helped her dig the ground, and together they cut the plastic strips that Nahla would make into tunnels to protect her plants from the cold. On the plains, they used similar ones for planting vegetables; they called them *plastic houses*. Nahla made dozens of small ones, and every plastic house formed one of the steps that she had dug into the mountain. She filled them with earth and planted different kinds of vegetables inside. Her husband was delighted; the war had made them all hungry. Then, day by day, her frame began to change. Ali saw how her back became different, curving over. She looked older than Humayrouna, whom he used to say was as old as the trees.

It was all taking shape in front of him now. Ali

saw Nahla plainly, wearing her lime-stained apron, putting her hands around her vegetables, picking up a seedling—it was only her top half he saw moving around, and he could vividly smell the wild thyme she used in her cooking. She used to mix her own herbs and produce dishes full of ingenious flavours, which they all gobbled down ravenously. One morning they found her building a tannour next to the tree for baking bread. She bought flour with the money she had earned from selling her plants and vegetables, and she began to bake their bread herself. She was completely independent of the outside world. Ali, like his siblings, couldn't stop watching her transformations. He would imitate the way she moved her hands, her wanderings—whatever she did, he would copy. He had no need to speak to her, and before many days had passed their movements were in total accord as they worked, accompanied by silence. Now she appeared as a phantom, indicating with a conspiratorial gaze the next movement that he had to make. The half of her that was waving to him swooped and planted a sprig of wild thyme in a rock, and then the rock started flying as well. She beckoned to him with a lime-stained hand, urging him forward, and as she scattered wild thyme the scent of it propelled him towards her. Nahla didn't talk—if only she would say something. Anything! Ali closed his eyes, trying to summon up an image of her from before his brother's death. But her image was immutable, fixed in the shape of her habitual leaps and balletic movements, her grim face, her dull, frozen eyes. He pushed on with his body and he could see her eyes now, although dusk had more or less fallen. He saw their emptiness. He saw her white fingers painting the house walls, gripping the edges of the coffin, and he knew he was seeing her in his mind, not with his eyes. He understood that she was gesturing at him to keep going, so he threw his body again until he lay one metre from the tree. He sighed and closed his eyes to see her more clearly, and Nahla smiled at him as she used to do before his brother died. Ali reflected that even if he didn't survive, at the very least he had to keep this promise to himself: to make sure his body stayed whole, so Nahla could see it and say goodbye to him, and so they wouldn't do to her what they had done at his brother's burial. He pushed himself, following her phantom, and before he lost consciousness again he knew that that these recurring blackouts might become permanent. In a burst of speed that began confidently, his head collided with the tree trunk and he heard a knock on the other side: the Other's head had also hit the tree, and he couldn't fight the blackout that was coming on.

As he closed his eyes, he knew that the being wouldn't kill him.

Chapter 12

The black seed, that blind thing, resumed dancing in front of him. It was a point of hatred he had come to know when they trampled on him.

Where was the tranquillity he longed for? All these memories and obsessions merely plagued him as he learned who he was.

He would never forget that day, when he first saw the black seed.

In front of the iron gate that opened up automatically, the old sheikh would tell him that everything here was opened and managed by means of a room full of screens connected to watchful cameras—everything in the castle was done this way, from opening a window to watering the plants. The sheikh would tell Ali that he was going to see something he had never seen before: something they called tiknulujiyya, which was operated and monopolised by a small kumbyutir, itself supervised by a specialised engineer. Ali was shivering as he passed through the entrance gate (although less than he was shivering now, while dreaming of flying up to the tree branches). He was with the old sheikh, who was absorbed in all these explanations while Ali gazed around him, utterly stupefied by what he saw, and uttering a furtive "Ya Allah" under his breath. He had only ever seen Zayn's palace from the outside, even though it was no more than a ten-minute walk from the village. He usually forgot it existed altogether. This palace defied explanation, and was surrounded by fear, dread, mystery, and power. What had happened to cause them to open the gates of their palace to him, and to others from the village? Why did they perpetually offer up so many sacrifices? Where were they? Who were they?

Ali walked alongside the old sheikh as they were preparing the rites for Eid Al-Ghadir, the feast of mercy—the day the prophet Muhammad took the hand of his cousin and son-in-law Ali and raised it up, saying, "If I am someone's mawla, then Ali is also his mawla." This is what his sheikh had taught him. By that point, Ali and his sheikh had become inseparable, and the sheikh had insisted upon Ali attending the Eid with him. The sheikh saw the opening of Ali's soul and grasped his faith; he had watched Ali grow up, and observed behaviour that he was not used to seeing in the boy's contemporaries. For his part, Ali liked to think that the sheikh of the village was of the same kind as his beloved saint in the picture, whom he had singled out since he was very small.

The world he saw inside the palace walls was dazzling. He could never have imagined such a place existed, not even in his dreams. The only way he could describe its splendour was "unreal." Trees were distributed around the huge building, unfamiliar trees he had never seen before—some dwarfs, some huge. He learned some were Japanese, others were tropical, and they appeared in many different shapes and sizes. He saw three date palms. When had they had time to grow here? The sheikh said that Zayn had brought them here already fully grown. Ali choked as he imagined it: three date palms, uprooted and laid out like corpses. He felt depressed as he looked at them. An image of their tall trunks was reflected in a huge wall of glass that seemed unusually tough. It was a wall no living thing could get through. Only light could overcome it, he said to himself, and he pressed his lips together so that he wouldn't turn pale or show any emotion. He had begun to gain control over his temper; it was part of his training, in preparation for the new world that awaited him imminently.

The villagers had started to see Ali in a different light. He was still an eccentric, but there was a growing element of tolerance and reason in him. He displayed a sage courtesy that seemed like a species of madness in times of war, when fighting and screaming and rancour erupted for the most trivial reasons. Ali, on the contrary, only grew calmer and more patient, so his sheikh said. In his conversations with the sheikh—which were really more like lectures—Ali used to maintain a strange tone, and the men started to hold him in high esteem because the sheikh had chosen him to serve the maqam. It wasn't important for the servant of the maqam to be a learned man, or a man of religion. Ali's first step would be to capture the sheikh's heart, and push him to teach Ali the principles of his religion.

The old sheikh of the village was one of the few men of religion who had remained in the mountains. These figures spread the learnings of their religion both to strengthen their relationship with nature, and to pass on the ways in which their forebears in the mountains had lived for generations. The old sheikh enjoyed the sincere respect of the people of the village; he would marry them, divorce them, resolve their problems, and they turned to him time and time again to manage their difficulties. He was no miser, though he was fairly poor and was subjected to ridicule by those sheikhs who had appeared in more recent decades. The old sheikh had acquired his reputation and his respect over a long period of time; he believed that he was responsible for each one of the villagers, even though he and many sheikhs like him had lost their spiritual authority and social standing. Their authority had been transferred to the new sheikhs, of whom Zayn's was one. But people's respect, their esteem for the sheikh's religious lineage, and the personal relationships that went back decades, were never forgotten. He used to tell Ali that the souls of the believers would ascend in each of their successive lives, until they finally reached their great light. He would say that Ali would soon fully comprehend his religion, and then the time would come for him to learn how to lead a virtuous life, and how to exist in the service of good. "God is in your heart, Ali! God is everywhere," the sheikh would often say to him.

Simply put, the sheikh had gained possession of Ali's worlds, and so he made no objection that day when his sheikh invited him to Eid Al-Ghadir at the palace. Zayn had already prepared his offering, and his men produced two sheep and two calves. He also brought his own sheikh, whom Ali used to call the new sheikh. Ali's elderly sheikh said that, after all, they would be feeding the poor—he had his own logic that Ali didn't always understand. The old sheikh would say to Ali, "Let each of us seek out what he wants. Zayn wants power! Are we his Lord to judge him? His reckoning will come! What is it that we want at this crucial time? We want to feed those poor unfortunates." Ali was silent, but when he saw Zayn's palace, a black seed was planted in his heart. From that day onwards, it grew and grew, becoming the size of a chickpea, and settled deep within him. That day, he saw a mirror image of the blue sky and the clouds in the huge swimming pool, along with the trees and the strange plants and the colourful flowers. There were lots of men constantly moving around and carrying weapons, and Ali reflected that the whole experience was like the mythical stories Humayrouna used to tell him about castles and sultans. There was a dome in the middle of the castle that gleamed in the sunlight and dazzled his eyes; it was more beautiful than he could bear. The sun had turned it into a ball that blazed with colours and engravings and pictures, all overwhelmed by the colour blue. And that day, at last, Ali saw Zayn's face. He appeared with his sheikh, who was a few paces behind him, and they both greeted the elderly sheikh together.

Zayn was perfectly aware that most of the villagers had no love for him; deep down, they knew that their children were dying in his place, although they didn't dare breathe a word against him—they knew the reward that awaited anyone who stood in the face of him and his authority, both here and in the capital. Fear was part of their very existence. That terror was a complicated, intricate fear that Ali didn't fully understand, but on the day of Eid Al-Ghadir, he learned what it felt like for the first time.

A memory of Humayrouna came back to him. Some of the villagers repeated that Zayn's men had disappeared her after she spat in Zayn's face. Humayrouna, whom Ali felt he'd let down ... He had stopped looking for her after the third week. It seemed to him that he had seen her standing on the highest mountain peak and calling him; and once, their neighbour said she had spotted the old woman going down into the wadi and disappearing into the bush. Then, another time, he thought he saw her climbing the tree by the mazar, but when he searched for her he couldn't find her. Yes, he had failed her. Not just him, either; all the villagers had been absorbed in burying their children and feeding the ones still alive. He wanted to withdraw and escape from this garden, this orderly, ordered world where roses and flowers turned into green triangles and rectangles, and ugly trees were trimmed until they looked like walls, so that he couldn't catch their scent anymore, and he couldn't spot the branches, which he told himself had become imprisoned fingers. Opposite, at the corner of the large wall that hid the outside world and was about four metres long, he saw a large table holding a spread of all kinds of fruit, such as he had never seen before in his life. In front of the table there was a swimming pool, shaded by a stone canopy with a red brick roof. The longer he looked at the scene inside the palace walls, the more Ali's heart sank. He took the sheikh's hand and asked him to stop and think a little longer about why they were there. The sheikh was one of those rare people who could see what others couldn't; he perceived Ali's troubled breathing and the black spot in his heart, and he whispered to Ali that in bargaining between two inevitable evils, he had to choose the lesser one. The men were gathering by this time, so the sheikh moved forward and urged Ali to come with him. There was another place inside the walls, next to the castle, a small house with three rooms. It was where the servants slept, and Ali thought of his aunt who had spent her life there. He saw some women cooking, and he heard a mutter coming from one of the men watching them. Ali knew the women who came from his village. They resembled his mother in many ways, in the curve of their backs and their wizened fingers, though they did not resemble her in her obstinacy. He knew by then that women were not permitted to attend the religious festivals in case they weren't pure. This knowledge came to him after the incident at the other maqam; he knew that a woman mustn't be on her monthly cycle, because this was considered unclean, and she should not touch the offerings.

Ali infiltrated the crowds while the sheikh was occupied in tending to the sacrifices. The new sheikh was presiding over the Eid, while Ali's elderly sheikh had stepped forward boldly to oversee a fair distribution of the sacrificial meat among the needy families of the village, and for an instant Ali remembered what the sheikh said, and why he called this Eid "the Eid of Compassion." In all the times Ali had accompanied the sheikh to the religious festivals, he had never seen the elderly sheikh eat any food, nor take the portion of the sacrificial meat he was entitled to. His missions of distributing meat to the destitute were hidden from people's gaze because, as he used to tell Ali, "We must be careful to preserve what remains of people's dignity, even if it is only a small piece." So Ali understood why the sheikh used to steal away at night, away from the eyes of the villagers, to leave them that bag of meat.

Even so, Ali was worried.

Despite standing right in front of him, Zayn didn't cast a single glance at Ali. His eyes were roaming somewhere far away from the surrounding crowd. Zayn was wearing sports clothes, white trainers that blazed in the sunshine, and a white cotton T-shirt, and he moved among his men with total assurance as they milled around him. Their weapons glinted in the sunlight. As the weapons shifted in their holder's grip, their glitter turned into rays that were reflected dramatically onto the hedges clipped into green walls. Ali looked at the reflections and closed his eyes. He wanted to tell the sheikh there was no need for weapons on this blessed day, but he didn't dare. He was coming to understand why the villagers acted as they did and he began to taste fear, and he hated it. When the crowd slipped inside to pray, Ali was forbidden to enter, so he followed them and stood at a window to watch. Most of the men had disappeared inside, and a grave silence fell after the women entered the servants' house accompanied by two guards. Lost in thought, Ali wasn't aware of time passing.

Perhaps now, wounded and prone, he could hear that silence which reminded him of Zayn and see the fear in people's eyes, whether Zayn was present or not. It was rare they actually saw him, but his influence remained. The villagers had no choice but to hold him in awe and fear, just as they had his father in previous decades. Zayn could set in motion sheikhs and men bristling with weapons, men who held huge mobile phones, spinning them round among their machine guns and strutting among the people. Some of them came from the village, others from the neighbouring villages, more than twenty in all. Why did a man like Zayn need so many companions, what did they do with him, how did they live, and where did all this money come from? These questions weighed heavily on Ali, but he didn't want to make himself a laughingstock by asking. He was afraid to even go near the men; he felt as though they would swallow him up. They could inspire fear with a single glance, hard as stone, in which he saw their contempt for people like him. They behaved in marked contrast to Zayn, who spoke gently and courteously and greeted everyone with a smile, although he didn't look them in the eye; he didn't see them, even when he was among them, fulfilling his duties in burying their sons. That day, after Ali left the huge palace without bidding goodbye to his sheikh, he decided not to go back again. He was determined to keep out of Zayn's way; he didn't want to so much as see him.

That day felt like a celebration, removed from what was going on all around them in their remote mountain village. It seemed to be from another world, one where the war wasn't spreading through their cities and villages, in the north and south; as if, here, they were plunging into another war altogether, one that killed them from within, and thousands of their sons were dying from it. Ali didn't know what the truth was. Questions gnawed at him, and the uncertainty over everything he heard kept him awake at night.

Zayn's charm frightened Ali too; he projected the image of someone untouchable, in possession of everything he needed to keep himself far away from that place where young men ventured out to alive and where they came back from in coffins. He distributed portions of meat to each of the bereaved families to quiet their starving bellies, including Ali's family. It occurred to Ali that he was eating what was essentially his own brother's flesh—his knees trembled at the thought, and he asked for forgiveness from the Lord. That day the sheikh eventually forgot Ali in the hubbub and went into the castle with the men. Ali wasn't supposed to follow, but he was able to use the tightly packed crowd to evade the notice of the guards. Ali stood by the broad window; the curtains had been closed, but he managed to peer through a slanted chink in the middle. He saw the men joining hands, and then he saw a young man come in, carrying incense. This was the quddas al-bakhour—later the sheikh would tell Ali that he would undertake the incense rites himself in the next few years. Ali stared at the men as they held hands and muttered. He couldn't see very clearly through the small gap in the curtains but he tried to read their lips, even though the sheikh had told him that the uninitiated would be struck deaf if they heard their prayers. The blessed day of Eid Al-Ghadir was one of their twelve holy days, and was closest to Ali's heart; he dreamed of the day he would be allowed to enter with them. His limbs relaxed and he raised his hands as if he were holding theirs, then he closed his eyes, imagining himself lifted above the earth and flying alongside them, their heads close together and their bodies floating in a circle in the void. Then suddenly the circle was shattered by a roar: "What are you doing here, you little bastard?" The man came up to Ali, grabbed him by the hand, and pulled him away from the window. He threw Ali to the ground and stepped on his neck—Ali could see the front of his shoe, he didn't close his eyes, then he felt the muzzle of the machine gun on the top of his head. The gun was pressing into his head, the shoe was pressing onto his neck, and he was shaking. "Get up, and get out of here," said the owner of the gun and the heavy shoe that left a red mark on Ali's neck. Ali remembered that he was wearing a blue cotton T-shirt that day, and the gun muzzle had pressed so hard it almost went through his skull. He also remembered thudding onto the ground and staring up at the dazzling sky. (The sky hadn't been dark then, as it was now, as he lay here recalling that fall.) When he fell, he saw a man sitting next to the large table by the pool with a pistol next to him. The man had opened a kombyutir and was watching something but, seeing what had happened, he left his place, headed towards Ali at a run, and slapped him. At that moment, Ali remembered Humayrouna's face when Zayn's men threw her to the ground at his brother's funeral, and he was seized by a limitless terror. He learned what it felt like when fear froze the blood in your veins. He stood up and ran out of the garden, while behind him he heard the men guffawing with laughter and shouting out in ridicule. Ali even forgot his sheikh, thinking only about the muzzle of the machine gun. He saw the emptiness of his own heart and the seeds of hatred and resentment, which he called his blind spots, that sprouted into wicked thoughts. He ran and ran, even though he was out of breath, and as he reached the village they thought he was flying. He raced down the terraced steps then climbed up until he reached the rocky precipice, and there he stopped. Ali placed his feet on the very edge of the cliff and spread his arms. He saw nothing in front of him. He forgot about Eid Al-Ghadir, and the obligation of compassion between people. The mountains and the sky and all his surroundings disappeared. Eyes closed, he hoped that two small wings might sprout from his back, wings that would take him flying, so he wouldn't need tree branches to hang on to. He thought of his aunt, who had grown a pair of wings and flown.

He wanted to jump. He wanted to fly!

That same moment, he heard a distant scream: Nahla, who had followed him, was panting and shrieking anxiously. Ali looked at her miserably and took a step back from the edge. He wasn't thinking about the palace now, or even his sheikh, who was still with Zayn. His desire to fly off the cliff edge had vanished as soon as he'd spotted Nahla running towards him. He realised that the curse of mothers was not merely their love, but the ropes with which their love binds its object.

Chapter 13

At last the moon appeared!

He saw it as he rested his head on the tree trunk, and listened to the sound of insects all around. He flung his hands upwards. He had woken up a moment earlier and now saw that the moon was illuminating the tree. Strangely, it seemed to him that he could see more clearly in the darkness, and he had momentarily forgotten the being behind the tree. He couldn't hear any sound coming from the Other. He had stopped breathing, to gauge how close the being was, but he heard nothing apart from the sound of insects and whispering. He was familiar with the hidden kingdom of small creatures that scuttled around him. He imagined them to have become large and lit up by the moon, with arms that grew ... six ... no ... seven giant arms crawling in his direction. There was a pair of red eyes that he thought might belong to a locust; the moonlight had turned them into two blazing pits of fire. Then a black fly with blue wings appeared, and it grew and grew and he saw the veins traced over its transparent wings. He wondered if perhaps he had made some mistake, and he was seeing the sun, not the moon. He closed his eyes and rubbed the tip of his finger against the tree trunk, and heard the sound of scraping, and the sensation made him feel he was alive. The hidden creatures in the forest stirred at the scraping noise. He could feel them crawling over his body, which meant that what he could see was no hallucination—but these were not normal insects. He could feel them underneath his heavy clothes. Where were they creeping inside his body? They seemed like giants as they flew all around him, like monsters that would swallow him up, though he knew they were just insects. But the vision was stronger than he was. He mustn't be afraid, he had played with them in his arzal, and on his secret trips to the forest he had captured them, torn off their wings, and examined their bodies. Now, he was too weak even to imagine them or remember their names. Now they were bigger than he was. They circled him in the moonlight; he spotted their blazing eyes staring. He reached around the huge tree trunk and scraped the torn skin off his palm. When he brought it up to his eyes he saw the small black silhouettes of insects clinging to a deep wound. He hadn't noticed this wound before. Then he saw his body parts—they had fallen off and begun circling the tree. He spotted his severed heel, his feet walking further and further away from him, and, much to his surprise, his hands scaling the tree trunk. His upper half was wearing clean, smart clothes. Then he saw his father next to him. They were in the square, waiting for his brother to arrive from the city. That had been an exceptional day—a member of their family was going to university! He was wearing the same trousers he could see now, on legs that were chasing after the shirt sleeves swinging in front of him. Fingers appeared from the ends of these sleeves. He couldn't see his chest or his head. He looked to the right then the left—perhaps he would see the rest of his body—but he didn't see anything, not even a shadow. Then he raised his gaze to the moon, which was still full. So he wasn't going mad, his body had come apart and he was observing it dancing around him in pieces. But it wasn't him! Could he believe that it wasn't him?

The clothes flying around him on his various body parts were from that day. He had never had new clothes before; one of Nahla's talents was recycling clothing—in the same way that they reused food, soil, rocks, everything, even grief. On that day, his father stood proud and tall, discarding his habitual slumped posture. He and his middle son were waiting for his youngest. They had buried his eldest son a year earlier. Ali remembered he had been standing next to his father, who was intermittently bubbling over with unfamiliar phrases of happiness and excitement: his youngest son, the family's pride and joy, would not be forced to go and fight, he was going to become a doctor. He spoke to Ali as though to a stranger, referring to his son in glowing terms. Ali didn't mind. Even now, leaning his torso against the tree, his father hadn't occurred to him at all until he saw his body parts cavorting around in those clothes. There, a year ago perhaps, while he had been standing with his father in the village square, a rowdy crowd had gathered and Ali heard shouting. He saw their neighbour with his mobile held out in front of him, muttering something unintelligible. He was quite far away and so Ali went closer. As their neighbour was filming, another man pulled his sleeve and yelled at him to stop this mad gossip, the country was at war. At that point Ali's father grabbed him by the hand to stop him going any further. Then he remembered that Ali wasn't a little boy anymore, he couldn't beat him any longer, and moreover the people in the square were always watching each other. He was proud of his sons and he wouldn't let anyone doubt that his second son was truly a man, so he let Ali go and followed him into the crowd. The two of them could hear snatches of the conversations going on all around them. At first they thought it was a funeral for one of the martyrs. The sky was matted with clouds, and the mild weather had improved the mood of the troubled villagers. The world seemed cramped to Ali; the square was boiling with men from the army, men carrying weapons, children, women, the elderly, and he heard men reading out a page of some edict the state had issued, an edict about people who owned land in their village.

No one in his family owned an inch of land. They hadn't lost their livelihood from the decline in tobacco farming but from working as hired labourers for the landowners who owned the tobacco terraces. This edict that they happened to hear now had nothing to do with them but, even so, Ali looked in terror at their elderly neighbour who was being subjected to jostling and yelling and might be beaten. He would have gone back to his arzal and left all this commotion but his neighbour started crying and making some kind of speech while another man filmed him on his phone. The old man was like a terrified child as he spoke, informing the camera he had lost three sons, and he offered them up as a sacrifice to the homeland and the state and the President. Ali knew that his neighbour, whose sons had died on the frontlines, didn't own anything apart from some rocky land he had turned into terraces for farming tobacco. In his children's absence, and with the decline in tobacco farming, he had stopped working the land. Ali turned his face away; he didn't want to remember the day they buried his brother. One man shouted that the state had unjustly and aggressively decided to seize farmers' lands, using the excuse they were neglected, and then someone else shouted that it wasn't the state doing it, but a gang.

Ali tried to extricate himself from the crowd but his father pulled him back by his sleeve; they had to wait for his brother. Ali felt that these new clothes were uncomfortable, and a bad omen.

Winter had been particularly cruel that year, and three years had passed since the start of the war. Ali had accompanied his father the few times they managed to find work on the plains as day labourers. He hated the role of the oldest son, and therefore one of the men of the family. If it weren't for the men screaming at his elderly neighbour, he would have run. He didn't care about any of this uproar. The centre of the village was crowded and he wasn't far from the maqam. Men appeared, strangers, followed by cars. There was no Humayrouna to scream at them as she used to do, to offend them or be the target of their contempt. Ali stayed silent, listening to the farmers fight with one of the government officials, who made it plain that the cars lined up in the village square belonged to him. He declared that, seeing as the farmers were incapable of properly cultivating their land, the state would take it. One man responded, "Ya Allah ... we gave the state our children and our lives and now the state is stealing our land." Another screamed, "Thieves!" at the official, whose face Ali couldn't quite make out because he was short and surrounded by the other men. There were some women in the crowd too. Ali recalled that most of the people there only had small parcels of land and he had never worked for them; some of them even used to accompany Ali and his father to work as day labourers. He didn't want to hear any of this, but he went up to his elderly neighbour. His father followed and stood next to him, swelling his chest. The bus still hadn't arrived. A woman howled at the official, "Damn you, you took our boys and our land." Her husband grabbed her by the shoulders and dragged her out of the crowd, and the couple moved off. The old man continued filming himself, saying, "Wallahi don't disgrace yourselves, you thieves—wallahi, don't disgrace yourselves, you looters." Only then did the bus arrive, and Ali and his father had to catch it in order to meet Ali's waiting brother. They left the crowd and Ali didn't turn back to see what happened to their elderly neighbour, who by now was in tears. He and his father hurried to meet his smiling brother, and in that moment they were both flying from the lightness of their hearts—the father because he was proud of his son, and Ali because soon he would go back to his arzal and carry on working the small terraces with Nahla, and he would take off these suffocating clothes. He was content to leave the square and its hubbub behind him. Something of what he had heard threw him into a deep, crushing pit: seeing those men who were screaming, who were weeping, who were fighting among themselves, who were ridiculing each other; seeing the government official, and knowing what he didn't want to know, as if he were saying to himself *this is the business of people with land, it is nothing to do with me.* He was preparing to meet with the old sheikh to receive his blessing, and begin learning his religion from him. Ali reflected on the saint in the picture, the story of his life, and how he had lived alone with his books and his trees in his cell. He used to nourish his dreams through his ability to live inside his head, between limits that he did not understand, but which he knew made him angry. So he had been on the verge of aiming a punch at the government official who had brought cars and men in order to take the small, lonely strip of land their elderly neighbour owned. Afterwards he would have taken hold of their neighbour's hand and begged him to go home, away from the square, but he didn't do any of that. Ali remained aloof, unable to move, suffocating in the clothes that made him look like a man. It was a dark suit with a razor-blade crease ironed into it, over a tight-fitting woollen jacket that Nahla had also knitted.

Every detail of these clothes was clearly visible to him as his body parts danced around him, bringing back the memory of that day, along with his father's gleeful face. Then he thought, why was he seeing those damn clothes? He had no answer, whether it was a kind of death, or more a kind of living. If he should die now, then why was he seeing that crowd of screaming men who had lost their land and their children? Why did he have to see his father's face now? He shrank before this bad omen. Nahla's face had vanished, and his father's face had come back. He had never liked looking at it so he sought refuge in the tree, spreading his arms around the trunk as he leaned his back against it, wishing he could turn around, hug the tree, and climb. But that would be difficult because he could still see the different parts of his body everywhere, clearly visible in the moonlight and getting further and further away from him. Then his torso appeared, flying in front of him. He saw his limbs breaking down into even smaller parts, and making circumambulations around the tree. Did death take this form? Was death a transformation into fugitive parts, perhaps transparent parts that grew to resemble trees and soil? But the limbs he had kept for his body weren't transparent. Then his hands came closer to his chest and he closed his eyes. Terror stifled his breathing. His hands lifted him, though he didn't know if they were really his hands, and he opened his eyes again but kept his eyes fixed downwards, afraid of looking up in case he saw his head flying around. Instead he saw the moonlight reflected on his toes. He straightened his torso, but as soon as he managed to stagger onto one leg he instantly collapsed with his head lying on the trunk. His flying limbs disappeared. He looked around and realised he had been imagining them. He tried to turn his body and felt a sting in his missing heel, or a bite ... Perhaps small creatures were eating his torn flesh. Not long had passed since he had been wounded and already worms were eating him alive. Or maybe they were just his fears. So he twisted his body, put his face close to the tree, and at that moment he heard a sound, the sound of a turning movement behind him—it was the Other! He squeezed his face against the tree, pressed his whole body against it and looked up. The distance to the top of the tree seemed endless and he slumped in exhaustion. He noticed that the moon had drawn close to the mountain peak, and there was no scent of dawn. Most likely, so he believed, that scent was still some way off.

Chapter 14

But what was this? A tree branch?

It was a severed hand, glowing in the moonlight. It was two arm-lengths away from him. That was good—it wasn't too close. Drawing back in a single circular motion, he turned over to face the other direction. He thought he was awake but a hand brushed his shoulder and he looked at it. It was holding his own hand! A hand was on his shoulders and yet he could see in front of him both his own hands. This wasn't a hallucination—had he grown a third hand? His body slid onto the ground so the tree was above him. He spotted the moon, which couldn't slip out from the tangle of branches. Was this his hand or not? He took hold of his left hand and his right hand and squeezed them, then he pulled his hair, and he felt his face and nose, then he crammed his fingers into his mouth in among his teeth and moved them around calmly. They were all there; he wasn't delusional. They were real bones. He became aware of an open wound in his upper lip. *Coward*, he told himself. It was just a scratch, a small injury of the kind he was used to from leaping atop the rocky bluffs, and so he wouldn't give it another thought. Then he tried to bend to feel whatever came below his knees, but he was stopped short by pain and the smell of blood, so he planted his severed heel in the soil, picked up some leaves, and used them to cover it up. He was going to the climb the tree. The long-awaited moment had come.

He needed to determine the strength of the branch in front of him. He steadied his elbow, turned over, and pressed his belly to the ground. Then he crawled, and something stung him in the middle of his chest. He wondered how an insect could reach his chest through his heavy shirt. Then he remembered that he had opened it and fussed with his stomach looking for an injury. There was still no scent of dawn. When he reached the branch, he would have to button up his jacket so no insects could sneak inside. He had never been afraid of them, he was only afraid they would get inside his wounds. The damn stings were multiplying as if he had fallen on top of a hornet's nest. He crawled forward, reached out a hand, and grasped the fingers of the severed hand he had thought was a branch—he had forgotten about it. It was a real hand, not a tree branch, not even a figment of his deluded imagination. It had appeared in his hand, just like that! He encircled it like he did with branches, as if in greeting. It was the second hand he had shaken that day. He imagined mountains sprouting fingers that lengthened towards the sky and withered in the earth, and he saw himself as a stone statue holding a severed hand, and he wanted to blow on the statue to turn it to dust, but he couldn't. The stings came back in every part of his body and he gasped. Just then he remembered the despair he had felt on the day he heard a rattle in his throat before he gasped; now, he heard the same rattle before he regained his ability to breathe.

On that day he and his father were coming back from the citrus orchards when they were stopped at a checkpoint. The men at the checkpoint lined everyone up to examine them. The men got off the bus willingly and surrendered their identity cards. Ali was tired and all he wanted was to reach his arzal after a long day's work. His cracked hands were sore from wielding the shovel. That morning Nahla had protested against him going down to the plains with his father; she wanted him to stay in his arzal. Perhaps she had known? He thought that she must have guessed everything that would happen afterwards. Perhaps that was why she leapt around them, furiously hurling things in their direction, even her husband's clothes! She didn't prepare breakfast for them as she usually did. She was staring at the sky and muttering, louder than her usual incomprehensible mumble, that her son should go to the maqam because the sheikh was waiting for him. She circled father and son as they were busy getting ready to leave and announced to the sky that Ali was going to stay—she needed him to help her move stones to make a new terrace for planting tomatoes, and she needed him to dig the earth and bend the branches that would be fixed between the stones, and then he had to secure plastic sheets over them ... She muttered and muttered. Her words turned into something like a mumble, while she pointed to the sky and turned her back to them. All the while Ali's father insisted that they had to work that day. God was guaranteed to protect his son. They would both earn a double wage by working a double shift; he hadn't been able to find any work for a month. Ali didn't remember exactly what his father said, and in any case he also wanted to earn some money as his younger brother had already started his first year at university. He honestly thought that Nahla was being overly fearful. He remembered her terror when he lined up by the checkpoint. His body went rigid when they took him away. He turned to stone, just like now.

It wasn't the first checkpoint to have stopped the bus that day; they had stopped at another just a few minutes earlier. The militias that had appeared since the beginning of the war had the right to stop people, vehicles, and anything else that walked or crawled over the ground. Like many people from the villages, the plains, and the city, Ali and his father never knew who was behind these militias. The small bus was carrying some men from the mountain who worked as day labourers on the plains. They were used to these militias whose members said they were here to protect people from enemies and terrorists. They never stopped firing into the air when they were moving, and these gun-toting men would disappear people. Once, the owner of a sports car vanished, and people saw his body flung on the road later on. His car had disappeared along with him, and the villagers knew it had been stolen. If these men stumbled on valuable prey, they would simply kidnap whoever was driving the car, steal it, and ask for ransom money from his family. Ali found it hard to distinguish between the militia checkpoints and the Mukhabarat checkpoints and the army checkpoints and the police checkpoints. Even the criminal gangs that stole and murdered appeared in the form of checkpoints. The world seemed mined with checkpoints that popped up and vanished, popped up and vanished; their common denominator was that the people manning them all carried weapons. Ali used to see the checkpoints on his way to work with his father, and he could never have believed that he would someday be standing in front of one, turned into stone. Aside from them requesting identity cards and searching the bus, he hadn't expected anything else to happen. On past occasions when he had gone down to the plains with his father, he had handed over his identity card without the least hesitation. He was thinking about the wages that his family would now have, thanks to him. He stared into the faces of the men from the checkpoint; they were human, like him, perhaps from one of the neighbouring villages. He was summoning up that memory, because then, like now, he had been on the verge of choking while his father spoke, saying that his first son had been martyred and this son would soon be conscripted, and of course he would gladly join the army, but just now they had to go home. The rest of the men were silent, apart from one who said, "Ya rajul, all our kids are on the frontlines, leave him in the Almighty's protection." Ali's father looked at Ali, and Ali looked at the men, and he thought this must surely be a dream—he would escape from under their noses and run as far as he could, he would climb the mountain and disappear in the forests. He wouldn't turn into limbs like his brother.

He wouldn't let them take him to die in Zayn's place.

He was on the brink of running. He thought about their weapons. He remembered telling himself that he wasn't a coward to be led like a lamb to the slaughter.

But what happened next stopped him.

He could hardly believe his eyes when his father grabbed one of the checkpoint men by his shirt and begged to be taken instead of his son. He had never seen his father like this: his voice was loud and unsteady, his words boomed, he seemed much younger all of a sudden. The men looked at him expectantly. One of them was angry and glanced at him in disgust, another grabbed his father by the shoulders and flung him so he fell on the ground. Then Ali's father crawled and knelt at the feet of the man who had thrown him down. Ali knew the checkpoint men didn't raid houses and carry men off to war. They didn't need to; they just hunted them down on the roads. There were videos constantly playing on state TV channels about enemies who killed and massacred, enemies who lived among them, and this was guaranteed to make many enthusiastically volunteer in self-defence. As for Ali, he had thought that day, when they were stopped at the checkpoint, that he would instead devote himself to looking after the maqam and learning his religion, forgetting all about the war.

His sheikh was confident that Ali was ready. He had seen the earnest look in the young man's eye as he sat in the maqam, gazing for hours at a time at the picture of his favourite saint. The sheikh regarded Ali as a wise and compassionate youth, his eccentricities notwithstanding, and he had decided to teach him the secrets of his religion when he grew stronger, when the time was right. Ali, who had turned over the idea in his head, was thinking about Humayrouna's house and how we would revive her memory. He would turn it into his own house in the days to come, and he was planning to restore it and clean it until it was time to read some of the books that the sheikh had given him. He didn't take much notice of the sound of the planes, or the wails of the mothers, or the quarrels among the villagers. He didn't sympathise with their elderly neighbour, or stay by his side to protect him from the pushing and shouting. He even seemed content in recent weeks, after that incident; he had succeeded in making his mother smile when she saw the flower on the aubergine he had planted in the plastic-roofed terrace—he had seen her smile! His satisfaction was complete when his brother enrolled in university, and when he discovered that his young red-haired sister liked sitting under the tree and reading for hours. He found a new enjoyment in listening to her. It occurred to this sister, who had suddenly grown up that summer, to read aloud from time to time, and he liked to listen and would even urge her to do so, and she would keep reading aloud until evening fell. Frowning up at the sky, he would listen earnestly in anticipation of the words that would come next. He thought his world was complete, perfect, that summer—the same summer he was stopped at the checkpoint and his father kissed the hand of one of the checkpoint men. Two of them had seized Ali and another was screaming at his father, calling him a coward because he wouldn't gift his son to the nation. His father replied to the checkpoint men that he had already given the nation a son as beautiful as the crescent moon, that he and his entire family were loyal to the President and the nation, but they had to let this son go. It suddenly dawned on one of the checkpoint men that Ali hadn't spoken and was moving with the obedience of a mystic sage who expected nothing. One of them, the one who was trying to lift Ali's father by the shoulders as he was kneeling before him, said, "Your son looks like he's received baraka." The father replied fervently, "It's true, I swear to God, he has, he won't be any use to you ... Wallahi, sir, this son of mine is an idiot, where do you want to take him?" And again, he kissed the man's hand and wept. The men just laughed and his father crumpled to the floor. When he saw that, Ali walked forward, dragging along the two men who were holding him, all without uttering a word. He took pity on the man his father was kneeling in front of, who was saying they were just following the law. But his father wouldn't stop begging, so Ali firmly spoke two short phrases as he walked forward: "I'll go with them. Go back to the village now." He seemed like a mature, rational man to the others at the checkpoint. Everyone—the men lined up, the women and the children watching from inside the bus—looked at him, full of approval for the young man who understood his patriotic duty. Overwhelmed with misery, Ali raised his head and gazed at the grey sky. He didn't say anything else.

He didn't turn back to look at his father, abandoned by the side of the highway after the bus departed. He expected his father to rise from his knees and go back to the village. Ali was confident in what he had done. It no longer mattered to him that he was going to a place from which men came back in coffins, it no longer mattered to him where he was, to the point that he even forgot which direction he was walking in. He went ahead of the checkpoint men, after asking politely to be allowed to walk and get in their car by himself. The checkpoint men rolled their eyes; to them, he seemed calmer than the occasion really warranted, as if he was playing the hero. One of them stopped him as he walked with his back resolutely turned to his father: "Hey, where are you going? The car's this way."

Ali turned around and saw the car that would make him vanish from his father's sight. His father appeared, standing in front of him, and they stared at each other. His father straightened his back, panting, watching his son closely. His feet had arched and spread and his arms were open in a semicircle, as if he were about to spring.

The distance to the car seemed to grow further with every step. Ali's eyes clung to his father's face, his head turning as he walked. Even so, as his head disappeared inside the car, he was able to catch a glimpse of something he was seeing for the first time in his father's eyes—that look, he thought, was love.

Chapter 15

His hand was still rigid. He thought he was coughing but he was spitting blood. He heard an echo, then woke up a little and turned his body over, and the hand slipped from his fingers. There was a sound of leaves shattering, accompanied by a movement behind the tree—it was the Other moving, standing up, twining himself around the trunk perhaps. He turned onto his stomach so that he was facing the trunk. The moon was right above him, he didn't need to make any movement to see it, a spongy moon shot through with veins that changed every time he caught a glimpse of it. He knew every variation in its colours. Today the colours seemed blue and grey, the sky was clear, the stars unchanging as ever. A little earlier it had seemed to him that he could see the stars falling around the moon, whose contours began to shift. It came right up to him and overwhelmed him, then it moved away to become a star, came closer, moved away again, like a bouncing ball. He had always thought it was bigger than that. Its round bulk disappeared and its edges seemed ragged, then it grew smaller until he could hardly see it at all; it was a faint gleam, melting little by little. He realised it was his eyes that were bobbing, that the moon was the same as ever. His eyelids lowered, darkness fell over everything. He didn't have the strength to keep his eyes open.

Here he was, swinging in doubt, uncertain whether he even existed. As if he was circling round and round. No sooner did he reach his longed-for goal than he was setting off again from the starting point: the moment when he first woke up, when he didn't know his own name. The starting point and the finish line were the same in his head. He tumbled and fell into a chasm, then rose and was lifted to the peak, dragged by an unseen assailant who had seized him by the heart, and he woke again to a vision.

Where had the strength come from that had brought back this vision? It wasn't a vision exactly, more a fleeting image: his father standing with bowed legs, looking through the water in his eyes at the patrol who had seized his son. People give that water different names, but it emerges from the cracks of their eyes, or wavers there, or it remains imprisoned and returns to the heart and kills it, or to the brain to convulse and crumble it. That day, Ali saw the water imprisoned, and he recognised the look that he had never obtained from his father before. Ali was afraid and his stomach quivered. Now strength returned to him and he tried to open his eyelids. From the experience he had gained over the course of this long day, as long as an entire lifetime, he knew he was going to black out. He had lost his ability to do anything other than sense that he existed. Existence returned to him with the phantoms of his father's gaze, but his existence depended on what he felt in this disappearing moment. He could not feel his fingers, or move any part of his body, and here he had seen the moon. Perhaps that was enough. An image came back to him of the deep hole he had seen himself going down, and he wondered once again whether it was his grave and if he really had died, and everything he had been looking at that day was just a delusion. He could no longer distinguish between dreams and delusions, between memories and the present. That brief glimpse of his father had muddled him. Then he realised that something would make him able to see his surroundings: even his delusions he would be pleased to see. He saw himself taking hold of the severed hand and throwing it as far as he could while he fell into that cursed grave he had seen at the beginning of the day. He had forgotten that he had seen himself in a hole, and that the hole was his brother's grave. Even Nahla's face had vanished now, and he thought again that he was just a pair of eyes. A light breeze blew and wafted a familiar scent—the scent of dawn. The moon was casting violet shadows over everything, and it gradually dawned on him that he knew that smell. It was one of the daughters of the wind, as he called them. He felt revived. He breathed in deeply and opened his eyes a crack, and saw his eyelashes like giant black bars in front of him. In this way, slowly, he opened his eyelids. He was flooded by the moon—it was large, clearer than it should have been, and unlike his usual moon, whose movements and trajectories he knew. He had memorised its phases and its transformations, and used to think that he was closer to the moon than the rest of humanity. This moon was raw and tender, clinging to the very tip of the oak tree, and it was illuminating his surroundings. This was it then; the moon was here for him. He returned and forgot himself for a few moments, then once again realised that the moon had come to him.

But the moon wasn't close, as he had thought—it was the tree! The moon was stuck at the top of its branches, and he was looking at them both. He thought he'd been sleeping on his front, close to the tree. But he realised the truth after a few seconds—he had been sleeping on his back, and the moon was clear and coming close to him, lighting his way. In the past he had always been able to climb aboard the moon and turn it into different shapes. When it was a crescent he knew how to shift his body on top of it, and when he was sleeping in his arzal and the branches hid its light, the moon would cheat them and move his body. He would close his eyes and rock back and forth and say to the moon, "Here you are!" He would urge the moon to race in the sky and it would raise him up—but the moon was full now, he couldn't swing on top of it. It occurred to him that if he wanted, he could cling to his mountain peak above his arzal, addressing the moon. If only it had occurred to him to swing on top of it when it was full, it would have thrown him to the furthest star. He had imagined the moon to be spongy when full, watery and airy when crescent. People were mistaken when they said the moon was silver, and equally so when claiming it was white. Ali thought it was blue, and it was the sky that gave the moon its colour, not the sun, as he had been taught at school. Sometimes he could clearly see its distant elevations and thought someone was looking back at him. How often had he thought this moon was just a fantasy, just a large light with no colour, shape, smell, or taste. He didn't believe what he had been told about the moon, what he had heard or seen on the television. Of course those few times when he was forced to watch television with his siblings he hated it. And he didn't much like the mobile phone that his brother had acquired for him either. Ali preferred his arzal. He saw it as a different kind of television, with a larger screen that looked out over the whole universe. He could place his finger on the deepest point he could see, where the sea met the sky, and where a small piece of the sea glittered as he was standing in his arzal. The moon used to come to him; their house was the moon's neighbour. He would gaze in contemplation at that strange space reflected in the surface of the sea. It seemed to sparkle like a mirror lighting up the world for him from afar. This mirror, formed at the end of the horizon, was the screen he called his own private television. He used to tell himself that one day he would go there, to the furthest point of the horizon. It was one of his secrets. In general he never revealed his secrets to anyone, although he had shared a few musings with Nahla and Humayrouna. For a long time he kept his thoughts and his questions inside a locked box, and now he was inside the box: his head.

He happened to turn and his eye fell on a pair of feet in front of him—the feet of the Other. He couldn't tell from the feet whether the heel had been severed, but there was one sound leg and the other was hidden behind the tree. The moon would no doubt light them up. He took a deep breath, determined to turn onto his stomach and not look in the opposite direction. He turned his body over, and fell on the ground. He felt as though he were flying, flying and falling. His mouth filled with dirt and the remnants of branches scratched his eyes. It was a hard fall that he hadn't accounted for—he had believed himself to be too weak to move his body with such force. So he sprawled on the ground and crawled forward on his elbows, hearing the leaves crushing beneath him and an inexplicable tumult on the other side of the tree trunk. He paid it no attention. He decided that any creature that came near him now, he would tear apart with his teeth. He gritted his teeth. He still had some strength—otherwise how could he have flipped his body with such force? He noticed he had lost the moonlight. He couldn't see it. He knew that the blue light all around him meant that the moon was still on top of the tree, and he was waiting to move forward. If he moved towards the trunk, the branches wouldn't let anything he saw be illuminated—in other words, when he reached the tree trunk the branches would hide the moon. This moon had fulfilled its task, he said to himself, just as he had done on the nights he decided to slip away from his arzal and wander the forest all night until dawn broke.

He moved forward a little and so did the Other. He went back and heard the same movement. Despite the darkness he saw the motion of the insects that circled him. He saw their black skulls as they made that noise, while their delicate legs roamed over the leaves. He felt stinging on his stomach. So, he was fine. And it was no use thinking about the smell of blood, or his severed heel, or other wounds that he still knew nothing about, but which he suspected were superficial. He was shaking and sweating, and he felt he was going to explode, boiling and bubbling and fizzing. Why didn't anyone come to rescue him? Instantly he dismissed that thought from his mind in case it made him stop trying to climb the tree. He remembered that he had seen an aeroplane circling overhead, that he had been looking at it the moment the bomb fell.

But why didn't anyone come to save him?

He chased away his suspicions and told himself to stop. Lips quivering, sweating, he scolded himself again. He didn't want to even touch the site of burning pain in his ear just then. Probably it was just a scratch. He brushed his fingers over it lightly then left it alone. If he spent any time on that deep, familiar pain, he would discover that his ear had flown away with the mistaken bomb, just like his heel. But he wasn't even thinking about that now. He had to be a man, and he still had his teeth, which he resumed gnashing.

With these teeth, he would rip up anyone who came close to him. He would devour them, he would tear at them like a hyena gnawing a corpse.

Now, he had to embrace the tree trunk, then move forward. He did so, and when his head bumped the trunk, he relaxed and heard something strange. He flung his hand up and grasped the trunk, hugged it, and passed his fingers over the rough bark, before struggling onto his knees. He was half standing now, and all he had to do was reach his arms out again. He seemed like a giant formed from soil and leaves. He raised his hands, bending the branches, and as if giving birth to himself, another person, whole and healthy and with full humanity, he emerged from his body. He touched the closest branch. The branches weren't moving, although as dawn drew near it was usually accompanied by a delicious coolness in the mountains, carrying gentle breezes that stirred the leaves. These branches he wouldn't expect to move because they were too large, but the leaves weren't moving either—he found that odd. He realised he was gripping the branch and he saw other branches in front of him; he saw their roots in his head and in his heart, just like that complex map of an anatomical cross section in a book he had read at school. He had always known that roots carried him to branches and that he was able to be part of them, although he hadn't consciously thought about it. He would just do what he always did. It made him feel that the strength suddenly bursting forth in him was a bed of tree roots that picked him up and shook him at night. He raised his body, took a firm hold of the tree trunk, and climbed up like a lizard scuttling over a wall. Even though the burning pain had grown out of control, erupting from his heel, exploding in his head, and lying distributed around his ears, he cleaved to the tree trunk as if he and it were glued together. Then he heard a familiar sound from the other side.

He ignored it and reached the fork in the trunk. He wasn't shaking. He drew a deep breath and stretched his body, then raised his hand and groped along the first branch that forked out. The moonlight still didn't reach him. The large branches remained some way from his fingers, further than he had imagined. He tried to pull himself up like a tree trunk, found he couldn't, and instead moved his body in a manner he knew, pushing his upper half ahead, stretching out his legs by bending his body and thrusting forward. As he performed this twist, his fingers and his thigh muscles slackened and he fell. He rolled with the force of the drop, turning over and over several times, and found himself again by the shredded sandbags, under the moonlight, looking at the tree that once more was far away.

He didn't know if it was the moonlight or his imagination, but he saw that the being had also rolled; moreover, he could see clearly now. Here, he heard a voice inside him: a clamour and a shrieking. He could no longer hear the insects, nor the branches breaking, and he couldn't see the full moon because his pupils had widened. He leapt up with his old acrobatic movement: he raised his hands to the sky, mumbled, shouted, then hunched over, ran clumsily towards the tree, opening his arms to catch the nearest broad branch that was his new goal. At that moment he still couldn't see his missing body strewn here and there; he couldn't see anything apart from the blue and the glow, blended with shining strands of light that shone clearly as they escaped from the dense tangle of leaves and branches. They seemed like the long, thin arms of gelatinous female beings reaching out and calling him. He grasped them with his fingertips, and threads of blue light broke through and lit up the air that had been stirred up by the movement of leaves and dust. The heel of his military boot was now clearly visible, open over a wound too deep and large to be termed *missing*. His heel was destroyed, the kind of wound that oozes blood slowly. He hadn't seen the blood, but it was spattered here and there in the violet rays of moonlight. He wasn't alert enough; drops of that blood had leapt alongside him and turned into rays of moonlight. As for him, he had sprung towards the branch, staring at it with stony eyes. He was about to fly!

The branch was reaching up high before him.

He threw himself towards it, not caring about the Other who was doing the same thing. His existence condensed in his arms that lengthened and spread out.

He was swooping onto his target.

He was holding the branch.

He was flying.

LERI PRICE is an award-winning literary translator of contemporary Arabic fiction. She has twice been a Finalist for the National Book Award for Translated Literature, in 2021 for her translations of Samar Yazbek's *Planet of Clay*, and in 2019 for Khaled Khalifa's *Death is Hard Work*. Her translation of Khalifa's *Death is Hard* Work also won the 2020 Saif Ghobash Banipal Prize for Arabic Literary Translation.

Book Club Discussion Guides on our website.

World Editions promotes voices from around the globe by publishing books from many different countries and languages in English translation. Through our work, we aim to enhance dialogue between cultures, foster new connections, and open doors which may otherwise have remained closed.

Also available from World Editions:

Breakwater
Marijke Schermer
Translated by Liz Waters
"A poignant story of love, autonomy, and the devastating power of secrets." —IVO VAN HOVE

The Drinker of Horizons
Mia Couto
Translated by David Brookshaw
"A rich historical tale that recalls Márquez and Achebe."
—*Kirkus*

Fowl Eulogies
Lucie Rico
Translated by Daria Chernysheva
"Disturbing, compelling, and hearbreaking."
—CYNAN JONES, author of *The Dig*

My Mother Says
Stine Pilgaard
Translated by Hunter Simpson
"A hilarious queer break-up story."
—OLGA RAVN, author of *The Employees*

We Are Light
Gerda Blees
Translated by Michele Hutchison
"Beautiful, soulful, rich, and relevant."
—*Libris Literature Prize*

On the Design

As book design is an integral part of the reading experience, we would like to acknowledge the work of those who shaped the form in which the story is housed.

Tessa van der Waals (Netherlands) is responsible for the cover design, cover typography, and art direction of all World Editions books. She works in the internationally renowned tradition of Dutch Design. Her bright and powerful visual aesthetic maintains a harmony between image and typography, and captures the unique atmosphere of each book. She works closely with internationally celebrated photographers, artists, and letter designers. Her work has frequently been awarded prizes for Best Dutch Book Design.

The cover photo, entitled *Dream Like* was shot by Mark Owen (Plainpicture) in Thame, near Oxford in the UK. The image was taken in a country churchyard on a misty morning. In spring and summer the leaves are out and create a beautiful walkway lining each side of the pathway, but when winter comes and the leaves have fallen, the trees look twisted and sinister. The raven in the tree caught the photographer's eye, and he crouched down and waited for it to take flight before taking the picture. Finally, the photographer added some texture from one of the gravestones to give the image a sense of mystery and foreboding.

The font used on the cover is called VOGA, designed by Charles Daoud and published by North Type, which is also the foundry. Charles Daoud's aim was to create an elegant and "sexy" typeface with unique letterforms based on the principle of contrast. These contrasts make it a glamourous display font for titles. To fit the type in the image and also have the image continuing over the spine, cover designer Tessa van der Waals removed and replaced certain details, like branches. She also slightly darkened some parts of the original image to increase the dramatic effect.

The cover has been edited by lithographer Bert van der Horst of BFC Graphics (Netherlands).

Euan Monaghan (United Kingdom) is responsible for the typography and careful interior book design.

The text on the inside covers and the press quotes are set in Circular, designed by Laurenz Brunner (Switzerland) and published by Swiss type foundry Lineto.

All World Editions books are set in the typeface Dolly, specifically designed for book typography. Dolly creates a warm page image perfect for an enjoyable reading experience. This typeface is designed by Underware, a European collective formed by Bas Jacobs (Netherlands), Akiem Helmling (Germany), and Sami Kortemäki (Finland). Underware are also the creators of the World Editions logo, which meets the design requirement that "a strong shape can always be drawn with a toe in the sand."

Printed in the USA
CPSIA information can be obtained
at www.ICGtesting.com
JSHW081951291223
54574JS00002B/3

9 781642 861358